DRENCROM

A NOVELLA

BY

HAMELIN BIRD

PIPER HOUSE

Cover Design, Interior Design, & Formatting by A.A. Medina | Fabled Beast Design

"On this sunken vale, we have freedom from contemplation. We luxuriate the ignorance of senses and choose absence of thought, will, desire, emotion. We eschew the banality of experience for thus is the sweetest escape, the unbecoming of ourselves. We crown alone the essence of nothingness itself, and strive only toward the ever-long respite of severance from the universe. Not to become one with all things, but to escape all things once and for all."

—Unknown

PART ONE

"Then came the discovery that adrenochrome, which is a product of the decomposition of adrenalin, can produce many of the symptoms observed in mescalin intoxication. But adrenochrome probably occurs spontaneously in the human body. In other words, each one of us may be capable of manufacturing a chemical, minute doses of which are known to cause Profound changes in consciousness."

Aldous Huxley, *The Doors of Perception* (1954)

First, the rush.

There's nothing like it, no matter what you've heard.

I'd read about it, hundreds of Reddit posts and more than a few flea-infested underground blogs. Then I'd taken up residence on the dark side of the web, if you catch my drift, and read a whole hell of a lot more. Then came the photos, documented evidence. Then, finally—videos. Verifiable, in your face. That's what pushed me over the edge. That's what made me take the leap. I knew I had to have it—whatever it took. Come what may.

There's this whole other world waiting out there, you know? Beyond the fringes, right out there on the edge. I'd seen enough to know. What can I say? I believed. And now, looking back, what can I tell you about it all?

I didn't know shit.

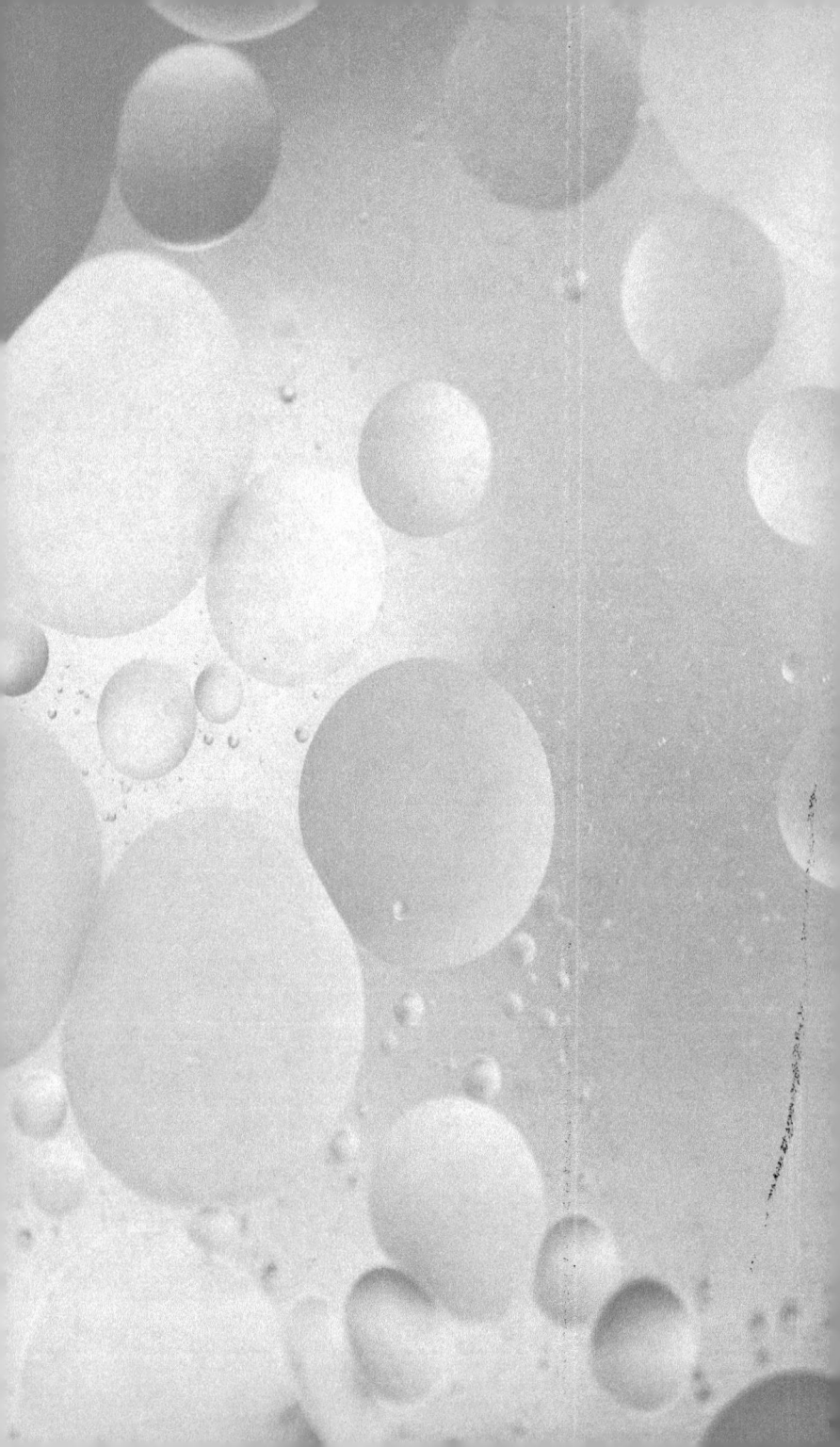

CHAPTER ONE

```
<SEEKING: DRENCROM>


   <CODA64: Anyone in Hagerstown CA area?
Ready for love. $$$>
```

She must've stared at the keyboard for an hour, waiting.

Outside the window, drivers laid impatiently into their horns, bleating like wounded animals in the streets below. The last of winter had faded, and tonight the temperature ran into the seventies. Everybody was on edge.

When she looked next, the responses had trickled in:

```
<SEEKING: DRENCROM>


<CODA64: Anyone in Hagerstown CA area?
```

Ready for love. $$$>

    <FRANKENFURT: Hagerstown, MD?>

    <2THETAN2: I'm Bakersfield>

    <XAN: Good luck>

Then, minutes later, another comment.

    <DROOGMANALEX: I'm near Hagerstown>

She stared at the screen, not believing. She typed, deleted, typed again.

The car horns blared, the night rushing warm inside her open window. A lather of perspiration had crept beneath her breasts, making her squirm in her seat. For such an ostensibly chatty person, she'd sure managed to clam up on herself.

She typed quickly, plunging ahead.

    <CODA64: legit/affordable?>

No sooner had she sent the response than her screen flashed:

DROOGMANALEX HAS INVITED YOU TO PRIVATE CHAT
  ACCEPT   **DENY**

She accepted the invitation.

Later that week.

Hagerstown wasn't the absolute best place to spend a Friday night, but this weekend was different. Tonight the temps had rocketed up to the eighties, the smog thick and heavy overhead, hovering like some invading spaceship as the worker-bees headed out for a night on the town. The smell of food trucks parked outside bars presently clouded the streets, and drifts of leftover confetti from that month's parade flooded the gutters.

On the outskirts of downtown, not far enough for the stench of bratwurst to fade from the breeze, Coda cranked the engine of her old Corolla, backing into the street. She punched her high beams and hit the gas, cruising toward Korova and past the thin crowd of horny losers outside Finnegan's Pub. A few bearded gawkers watched her go, dipping their sunglasses even though the sun had retired in a blush of stars beneath the horizon.

She'd keyed the address into her phone—a small little corner of a suburb at the western fringe of Arcadia.

Arriving an hour later, the house stood dark on the corner.

Her engine idled, the car halted in the street. For what seemed like a long time, Coda stared at the darkened eaves of the house—a nice house, she noticed, a *polite* house, so much more polite than her own, back when she stayed with her folks—until a window flashed suddenly with light and she let off the brake. Following their agreed-upon directions, she pulled around back, parking on a crumbled slab of concrete next to a corrugated tin shed. She eyed the shed, slivers of orange light bleeding through the slats of the door and touching softly at the ramshackle roof.

The yellow glow of a porch light sprang on, drawing her eye.

It was almost full dark now, the stars coming alive in the night sky as the back door opened and a young boy—perhaps ten years old, twelve at the oldest—ran out to the car.

"Whoa, kid," she said, popping the car in reverse. "Sorry, wrong house."

She'd started away when he reached inside the open window, revealing a small glass vial wrapped in shadow and blending with the night.

"Eight milliliters," he said. "Where's the cash?"

She stomped the brake.

"Are you fucking serious right now?"

"Hey, you want it or not?" He held out the vial, like it was candy. "Alex says take it or leave it."

She looked the little brat in the eyes. A strange look on his face—not anger, exactly, but stern.

"Not too much at once," he told her. "This your first time, right?"

"Tell *Alex*," she said, "I will have words with him later."

And handed over the cash.

She got home within the hour, put on some Garbage and Nine Inch Nails.

There was something in the air, a chill she hadn't noticed before, and she figured a bit of incense might do the trick. She lit a few sticks and went to the bathroom, relaxing her bladder as she drank down the vial.

She waited, lying on the couch, the smell of patchouli

filling the apartment. Sometime later she'd grown bored and walked down the hall to Ms. Wendicott's door. Ms. Wendicott had taken a tumble down the stairs the week before, and she figured it'd be neighborly to check up on her. Moments later the door opened and Coda asked how the hell was she doing?

"Oh, I'm just fine, dear," Ms. Wendicott said, speaking from behind the small steel cage of her walker. "Nothing that won't heal—would you like to come in for some Earl Grey? I've just put on some fresh?"

Coda did a little twirl in the hallway. "No shitting, I was just thinkin' how much I'd absolutely *adore* some Earl Grey."

Everything in Ms. Wendicott's apartment was old, all artifacts and things you'd find in a flea market. But Coda liked looking at it all, imagining what kind of person would make a doughboy soldier out of plaster, and what sort of person would see it and fall in love and think to themselves, *I've always wanted a plaster doughboy soldier, and with eyes as inexorably dead as these.*

"And this," Ms. Wendicott told her once, "is a harmonica from a merry-andrew of the Medici family. Can you believe it still plays?"

There were always mints on the table at Ms. Wendicott's.

"It's sure warming up out there, isn't it?" the old woman asked now.

"It's hot as hell, that's for sure," Coda said, plopping down on the old sofa she always sat in. There was an ancient gilded mirror over the far wall, and she could see just the very top of her head reflected back at her. Her dark, greasy hair, knotted and bushed like a desert tumbleweed.

Ms. Wendicott brought over the cup of tea, her warm

smile beaming down into Coda.

"Certainly you've got better things to do on a Friday night than visit with an old biddy like myself? Shouldn't you be off with a boy, or traveling out to the mountains? Lake Tahoe would be magical this time of year."

Coda laughed. "I'm pretty gay, Ms. Wendicott, remember? And it takes money to travel, so. Big nope on that."

She wasn't really gay, of course. She didn't know what she was. She hated most people, and couldn't stand others, and she wasn't sure where that left her. But the thought of some dopey man making moves on her made her sick to her stomach, so she supposed that counted for something.

Ms. Wendicott smiled, sipping from her tea.

"Are you still job-hunting, dear? I recall Mr. Hal in 4-C could use help."

Coda shrugged. "Meh. Little bit. Actually I just dropped this new kind of drug, I'm sort of waiting for it to kick in."

"Oh dear," Ms. Wendicott said. "It's not harmful is it?"

"No, not harmful," she told the old lady, staring at the bushel of black hair at the bottom of the mirror. "It's all-natural, just makes you sort of batshit for a while. Nothing dangerous."

"Just so you can make it back down the hall, dear."

They chatted awhile about Mr. Hal in 4-C, and how he'd probably be leaving earth in the very near future. He was housebound, and sickly, and recently they'd started him on some morphine capsules, and probably all those other meds they give people to make them all woozy before they kick the bucket. Coda had indulged more than a few choice words with the old fart, mostly banging at the ceiling with her broomstick and telling him to keep it down up there, and he'd bang right back and tell her to lick his stinky old ass. She loved that man, and would sorely miss him when he was gone.

When they'd finished their tea, Coda yawned and got up to leave. Ms. Wendicott had become something of a mother to her over the last year, and true to form, cranking up her old walker, she cruised over to the kitchen table, removing a few bills from her purse.

"Take this, honey," she said, holding out the money. "Go treat yourself to some ice cream."

Coda looked at the bundle of cash, knowing she'd feel bad later for taking it. But that didn't stop her from doing just that, pushing the crumpled bills down into her pocket.

"Thanks, Ms. Wendicott."

The old woman smiled pleasantly, and Coda gave her a hug, never taking her eyes from the ornate gilded mirror.

<CODA64: hey fuckwad. this stuff was a bust, I want my sixty bucks back.>

Alex saw the message, and felt deflated.

He should've gone with his gut, and gave her the good stuff. The stuff from last Halloween. But, since it was her first time and all, he figured he'd try out the stuff from the week before, and sure enough that had been a mistake. He'd been out of it that night, out of the groove. No flow. He should've known the yield would be dog-ass, but he'd wanted to believe otherwise.

Now he knew better.

```
<DROOGMANALEX: I'm sorry to hear>


<DROOGMANALEX: My bad—let me replace?>
```

He waited, thinking there wasn't much of the Halloween stuff left. He'd have to re-up soon. That meant a couple hours to himself—not an easy feat, nowadays. He'd figure something out.

His screen flashed.

```
<CODA64: if it's more of the same, I'll
pass>
```

He typed out a response, and she hit back with the obvious question. They went back and forth with that, Alex doing his usual tap-dance ballet.

```
<DROOGMANALEX: different batch, GUARANTEED>


<CODA64: okay where do you get this stuff
anyway>


<DROOGMANALEX: why do you ask?>


<CODA64: call me crazy, not sure i trust
somebody with GMAN in their name>


<DROOGMANALEX: haha fair enough>


<DROOGMANALEX: my uncle works for a bio-
```

medical corporation>

    <CODA64: and?>

    <DROOGMANALEX: that's all you need to know>

    <CODA64: toche>

    <CODA64: touche>

    <DROOGMANALEX: same time next week?>

    <CODA64: um how about same time tmw>

    <DROOGMANALEX: can't do tmw, next week soonest>
    <CODA64: ughh fine>

    <CODA64: and don't send a mfing kid out this time>

    <DROOGMANALEX: haha will do>

Alex closed his laptop, swiveling his seat to stare out the window.

Thinking, thinking. Putting together the pieces.

His room was dark, and turning back he slipped a hand into his desk drawer, fumbling blindly for the last pair of vials tucked away in back. Then he had them, eyeing his stash— fifteen milliliters, maybe twenty—and considered dosing himself then and there, just for the hell of it. He'd already dosed once, earlier that night after the girl had left, following her old Corolla back to the apartment building. He'd flown high as a demon through the clouds, and returning later he'd heard the front door opening, and hurried downstairs.

He wouldn't mind a repeat performance now, before sleep. But no, he'd better save it.

He'd need another yield like Halloween night, and a little pick-me-up for the occasion would go a long way in making things easier on himself.

He tucked away the vials and dropped into bed, remembering the cool rush of the clouds rustling through his sandy brown hair.

Alex was never the point, never even a blip on my radar. He showed up when he needed to, and that's all she wrote. I was off to the races, no looking back. We'd made plans for later that week, same deal as before. Everything was orchestrated, business-like. That is, we weren't criminals and didn't carry on like addicts. Because we weren't addicts, not really. I mean, maybe Alex—we'd only just met, what did I know?— but what I'm trying to say is that everything was very business-casual from the start. That would change, later. But I carried myself like a professional, and he'd done an approximation of the same, and we'd set another meet for Friday night.

I know what you're thinking: young woman, meeting strangers from the dark web at some random address. I get it, okay? But if you think things like that bothered me in the slightest, then you obviously don't know me so well.

I'll forgive you, this time, us only getting to know each other and all.

Just, you know. Don't let it happen again.

Meantime, after that hellacious bummer of an evening,

what I really needed was a drink...

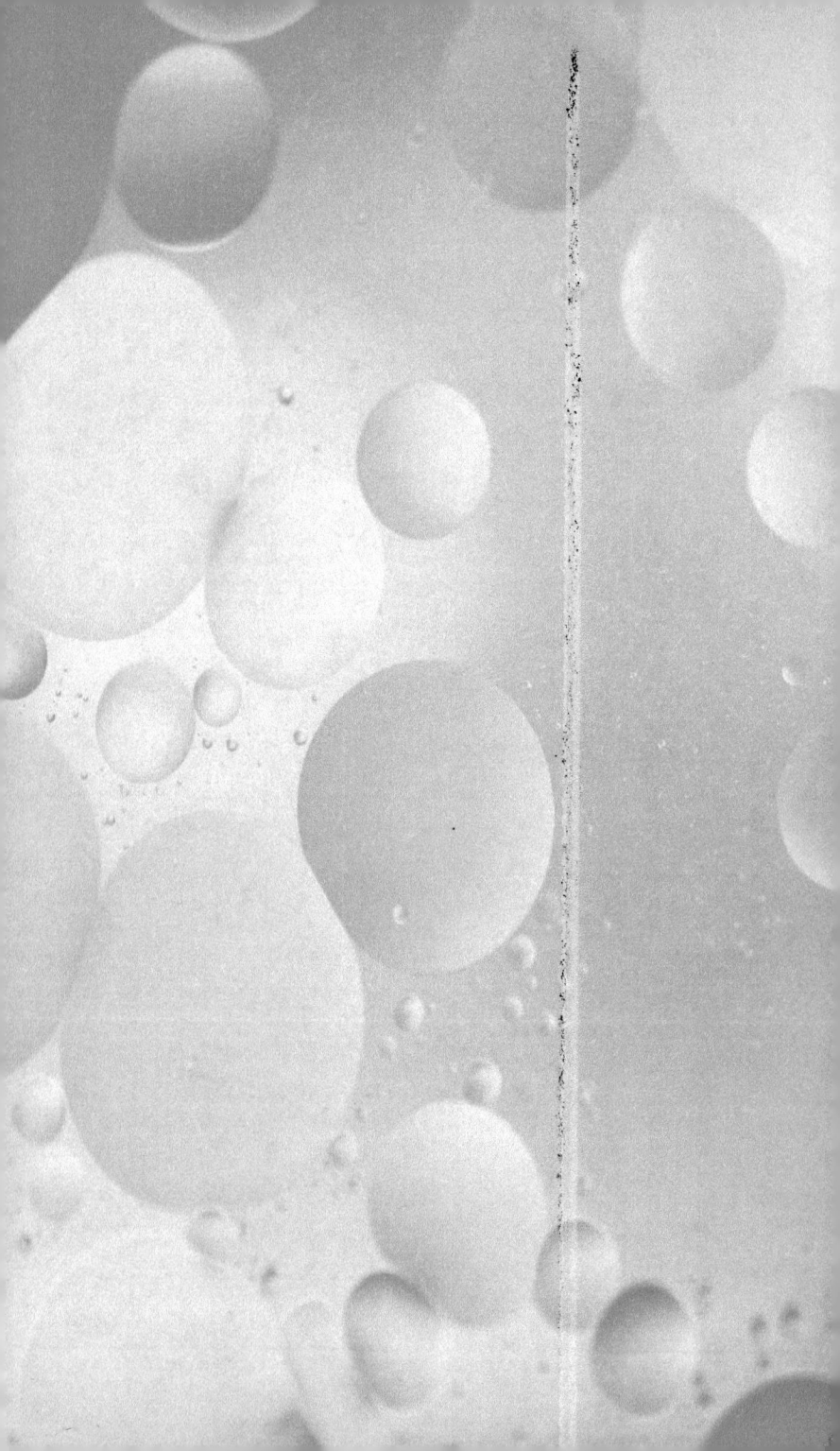

CHAPTER TWO

"Do you see any women doing that to each other? Ever? No, see, because it's the *guys* you got to be scared of. Thanks to the internet there are whole slews of perverts out there." The old man sipped mightily at his drink, wiping his mouth. "Men are an uncommon animal, you know? Do you have any idea, for example, what percentage of serial killers are young white males? A whole fucking lot of percentage. Who does the raping? The murders?"

Coda twisted on the stool, glancing over the late-night crowd.

She'd thought dropping a couple dollars of booze into her stomach might liven things up a little—ending the night, if not on a positive note, then at least a drunken one. Now, staring at this creep saddled up to the bar at Finnegan's Pub, listening to his drunken rant and smelling the gawd-awful stench of his boozehound breath, Coda wished she'd stayed at the house.

"Who are the ones going out staking people's heads and blowing shit up?"

Coda swallowed the last of her beer, leaned closer, and belched.

"Men?" she asked.

"Precisely, little lady," he said. "*Men*. Cold when they're cold, hot when they're hot. Meat heads with nothing better to do than go and pound the hell out of shit. Testosterone junkies. Serial-murder-rapist pigs so over the rainbow with rolling in their own shit that their heads might explode. Women are full of passion—yes, it's true—but at least they are semi-rational beings. Men! Men, these guys are asleep at the wheel. No clue, no desire for one. We could do anything and it would be nothing new. Now, I'd like to buy you a drink, okay? I'd like to hear your story, and get to know you a little. Why don't you tell me about yourself? Because, right out the gate, let me tell you, I don't judge. Age is just a number, okay? You don't know me, little lady. But it's a sick world, I understand. And I *do not* judge."

"Do you ever shut your fucking mouth?"

"The point I'm making is, I understand your position, and I empathize—"

"Listen old man, I don't care what your point is. Now you're starting to fucking piss me off, you need to zip it with that shit. I don't need you to *understand* me, okay? You are not my daddy and you're damn sure not my shrink, so I could give a flying fuck at a donut what you think of me."

He blinked. "I understand completely."

"You make me sick."

She scoffed without irony, pulling away from the bar and out into the slow-motion crowd of bodies, making for the door. She'd walked down from her apartment and started back now along the sidewalk, passing the closed shops and department stores. She'd kept the empty vial from earlier, and presently fished it from her pocket, running her tongue along inside.

At the end of Mackey Street she turned left past the park, steering clear of the group of adult kids who'd wandered down from Finnegan's and One-Eyed Jacks. They'd taken up residence at the jungle gym, giggling like fools and lighting firecrackers, shooting bottle-rockets.

"*Hey, Coda! Woohoo-look-at-this!*" one of them called, and Coda kept moving like it was pouring a rainstorm and she had to get home in a hurry.

She cut through Valley Plaza and entered the woods, swamped by shadows and the noise of the firecrackers fading at her back. She'd been through these woods countless times— but not lately, and tonight seemed like a damned lousy time to renew the habit. Her tongue lashed around inside the vial, a bitter taste filling her mouth.

"Stupid trick," she said, and tossed the vial away into the shadows.

She'd had a few fingers worth of whiskey back at the bar, and the farther she walked into the woods, the more unsteady her feet became. A sliver of moonlight shone against the ground, lighting her way through the trees. She watched her shadow, the bitter taste sinking into the pits of her teeth, and when she stumbled, her shadow stumbled, like a small dancer in the spotlight of the moon.

Many times she'd stood at Ms. Wendicott's window,

chewing those funny mints from her table and looking down on these woods. The mouth of the trailhead yawning against the surrounding darkness of the trees, like a bellowing black hole in the dark of space. Making her way in that direction, she imagined Ms. Wendicott at her window now, gumming those mints and gazing down, and considered what the old woman might think seeing her goose-limbed shadow skipping out of the woods. Like a Peter Pan doll, just skipping along thinking what a ditzy shadow-girl she was and how she'd better get back to Neverland, second star to the right and straight on till—

When she noticed the figure along the path, she stopped.

Her shadow stopped.

The shape was farther down the trail, kept back in darkness save for the crescent of a feminine face in moonlight. Not moving.

Coda broke into laughter, the whiskey still churning strong in her blood, channeling her anxious fear into something more closely resembling *shan't-give-a-fuck*. She pushed ahead, performing a whimsical stroll along the path, and when the figure broke suddenly from the darkness, heading in her direction, Coda refused to look. They passed in a place of shadow, the encroaching boughs of trees silencing the moon, Coda not looking up, not saying a word as a cloud of patchouli passed her down the trail. The sound of crunching earth beneath the stranger's feet faded at her back, dwindling into a sudden silence that was broken by the whistling of bottle-rockets and *rat-a-tat-tat* of more firecrackers through the woods.

When she looked back, the figure was gone.

Arriving at the trailhead minutes later, she glanced up, half-expecting to see Ms. Wendicott at her window after all.

Coda paused and smiled, waving like a model at celebrity photogs and gagging on the acrid aftertaste in her throat.

But the windows were dark, reflecting only the moon.

She looked closer, studying the sharp slivers of moonlight stretched across the glass, remembering the warm stench of the old creep's breath back at the bar.

For once, she didn't feel much like being alone.

Moving across the grass toward her apartment building, the sweet stench of pot suddenly rang clear as a bell and she hurried inside, taking the stairs two at a time up to her floor.

The door at the end of the hall was cracked open, smoke pouring from inside. Trent Modlin and Gaston Hughes, two dopes she'd met the year before, shared the place, and she spotted them now, poking her head inside the door.

"I can smell that all the way downstairs, ya know," she said.

"Coda!" Trent said, walking over. "Come in, the night is young..."

"Yeah, come on and get a free toke," somebody said, and Coda realized it was Cutty-something, one of those random faces she knew without knowing. Which was good enough for accepting free tokes, she assumed, and so made her way inside, crashing next to him on the floor.

When she'd taken her toke and passed it on, the bitter taste had eased off in her throat. She caught Trent's eye and said, "You ever come into any of that? What we talked about?"

He laughed, rolling his eyes. "Yeah, right. Sorry, I've already done it all."

She looked hurt. "Serious?"

"Hell no, Coda," he said, coming over and sitting next to

her. "That stuff probably isn't even real, forget about it."

"What isn't real?" Cutty-something asked.

"Forget about it," Coda said.

"Adrenochrome," Trent told him, and Coda punched him in the balls.

"Ow! Shit, stop Coda, only Gaston gets to touch my balls."

"Never heard of it," Cutty-something said, and pulled a baggie from his pocket. "Just got some banging tabs though, you dig?"

"No thanks," she said. "And are those pills? Ew, fentanyl much?"

Cutty-something made the bag disappear into his pocket. "Suit yourself."

"Did somebody just leave here?" she asked. "A girl, I think?"

"Bridgette was here," Gaston said. "She bounced for Tramell's, that was like two hours ago. Why?"

"I thought I saw somebody on the way over," she said, hefting the bong for another toke. "Through the woods, coming back from Finnegan's."

"What'd she look like?" he asked.

Coda lit the torch and held it to the bowl, and moments later released a rolling bank of fog across the room. The others coughed, playing it up for effect.

"Yeesh, Coda," Trent said. "Smoke champeen, over here."

"I don't know," she told Gaston. "I didn't see her face. It was dark."

"Maybe it was your doppelgänger," Cutty-something said. "Like, maybe it was *you* but *not-you*, ya know? Like in the comics, dig?"

She blinked back at him, restraining the urge to grab the bong and wreck it across Cutty-something's face, or rip the rings from his ears. "Wait—what's your name again?"

"Cutty."

"What the actual *fuck*, Cutty. Why would you even say that?"

He shrugged. "Can't see somebody's face, that's probably your doppelgänger. That's the way it works, right? Everybody knows that, it's like some Marty McFly shit. Because if the two of you ever met, the whole universe would crinkle up like a tin can."

"Monkeyshit," said Gaston.

"Kid you not," he said. "Einstein wrote that, that's what he said. He said the whole joint would crinkle up like dirty fuckin' tin can, dig?"

"Exact words, right?" Trent grinned.

"Ballpark," Cutty told him. "Or maybe it was Gandhi. It was somebody."

"Maybe she was your clone," Gaston told her.

"This girl," Trent said, offering Coda a puff from his menthol. "Was she as drunk as you are?"

She took a puff from the cigarette, handed it back.

"I don't know, she ignored me."

"Yep—sounds like you, all right."

"It's not funny," she said, snatching the bong.

"No, not funny," Trent said, apologetically. "Pretty weird, though. Hey—if you see her again, tell her I think she's pretty."

"Maybe," Coda said, and took another hit from the bong, fanning the smoke like perfume. "Thanks for the buzz, cocksuckers. I gotta roll."

"You just got here," Trent said. "Chill, hang out a little."

"Sorry, gotta run," she said, getting up and starting for the hall.

"Shut that door on your way out," Gaston called after her.

I'd be lying if I told you it hadn't bothered me.

Not that I believed all that doppelgänger jazz, not really.

It wasn't that. I'm not a total dumbass, okay?

Just, looking back, I realize now what was happening to me, what had started to happen. I realize that first dose hadn't really been a bust after all. It wasn't like the other times (nothing quiet about those other times) but it had reached out, touching me softly, feeling me out.

It had seeped down into me, a slow acid, and was building a deliberate empire somewhere deeper than I'd ever thought to consider. Beyond reason, in the wilderness places. The inner lights were shifting, casting new and different shadows along the contours of my heart. What can I say? Some days you walk around in a coma, and never know it. Sometimes you're so busy waiting on a thing, you can't feel it sneaking up from behind.

In those days, I was too busy to feel a lot of things.

Instant gratification is a bitch.

CHAPTER THREE

No sooner had Coda shut the door than Gaston Hughes hopped from his seat, moving to the kitchen to grab another cold beer from the fridge.

"Fetch me one of those, will ya?" Trent called.

Gaston returned moments later, handing off the bottle to his roommate and settling on the floor next to Cutty.

"All right, back to business," he said. But first, nudging Cutty with his boot: "Give me another tab, will ya?"

Cutty hauled the baggie from his pocket, fishing the tab from inside and handing it over. Gaston gulped it down with a swig of booze and sniffed, shaking his head, humming a sloppy speedcore beat.

"So, no mistakes," he said, turning a serious eye to Cutty Suggs. "This has to be clockwork, get it? I'm talking *smooth* as fuckin' *butter*."

"Smooth as butter," Cutty repeated.

"Oh god, not this again," Trent groaned, tossing back his head. "I'm gonna go take a dump, you fellas have fun."

But he didn't go anywhere, just sat there flipping through his stereo programming manual. Trent had taken an interest in the servicing and installation of home and car stereo systems, and had spent the last few weeks studying up for no discernible reason.

"What time do you get there? I mean, your ass in the parking lot?"

"Nine o'clock arrival," Cutty said. "Then wait for your signal."

"Wait for my signal," Gaston said. "Correct."

"Where should I park?"

"Anywhere," he said. "Why should I care where you park? Just, you know, not in front the windows, if you can swing it. Good?"

"Not in front the windows, sure thing."

"And who gets hurt?"

"Nobody."

"That's right. Fucking *nobody*."

Trent shook his head. "You guys gotta have better ways to scratch together some cash. Gaston, if your dad finds out—"

"He won't find out shit, okay? Cutty, you just stay super-fuckin-cool and we'll be right as rain, sweetheart. He'll just be glad I'm okay, that nobody got hurt. He'll be glad the windows weren't shattered all to hell."

What had given them this bright idea—see, earlier that winter some sad toothless sack had robbed his father's store with a pocketknife. Gaston hadn't been there for that one, but this guy Buddha had—a brickhouse Samoan who did night shifts. So had the girl-on-duty's boyfriend, a beefy linebacker by the name of Jeff Summers. They'd chased the man down, right into the parking lot and around the side of the store, and Jeff swatted the back of his head with a board. They called the police, and Buddha sat on the offender as they waited for the cruisers to arrive; whenever he came back to consciousness, Jeff would beat him back down with the two-by-four, smashing his face until he passed out. A puddle of oily blood formed beneath them.

"Yo, watch the shoes, homie," Buddha told him, crunching lower on the man as they waited for the cops. "Aim somewhere different next time, you're ripping his scalp all to shit. Motherfucker's blood is gonna get on my shoes, my brand-new motherfucking *shoes*."

Gaston's father split what the perp had stolen between the men, since they played heroes and he would have lost the money anyway. He'd even tossed a couple hundred to Chandra behind the register.

This would be the same, only different. This time the escape would be swift, and successful. Gaston would make sure of that, primarily due to the fact that he'd be the guy behind the register, the guy fumbling with the phone to ring up the cops. He'd be the guy handing over the cash.

"I really need this," Cutty said. "I'll be able to go to treatment—*professional* treatment, not that court-ordered garbage—and get my life straight. Then maybe I can get my own place, hold down a job, everything."

"I'd hire you at my stereo shop, if I had one," Trent said, flipping another page. "You'd be in charge of subwoofers."

Cutty shrugged. "Gotta be better than begging."

CHAPTER FOUR

Her fifteenth summer had been a revelation.

On those long summer nights she'd lay on the sand outside her parents' beach house and stay up late listening to Joan Baez and Janis Joplin, reading Ginsberg or Rimbaud. One of those nights she'd fallen asleep beneath the stars, and had dreamed she was a traveler along that same road. Some beautiful bohemian know-nothing in rags with a gypsy sway and she never stopped in one place too long, never let the grass grow tender under her feet.

That next year she'd moved on to *Jagged Little Pill* and Kerouac, Basquiat and the Marquis de Sade, and by then the script was written. She'd started behaving erratically—okay, she'd admit it—and things started moving real fast, life exploding like a champagne supernova in front of her own dark-rimmed eyes. She'd got in a bit of a fender-bender, the kind that totals cars, and her parents hadn't been too happy about that. But then her parents weren't too happy in general, so what else was new?

She wished she could meet her own Dean Moriarty, or Zelda Fitzgerald, and the two of them would roam the prairies till the sun went out like a candle, till the wheels fell off and the starless night of some rugged post-world wrapped them warm like a blanket. They'd be heathens, scraping a living from the barren earth and making love between the rocks, nodding off in fever dreams beneath a nuclear-winter sky, choking on their vomit as society crumbled to a forsaken wasteland of desire and then even that was swallowed by the rearview mirror.

The road went on forever.

Knocking on the door of apartment 4-C, Coda wondered at what hellacious pitstops she'd never imagined along the way. She should've known, she supposed. Zelda Fitzgerald (47) ended tragically in a mental institution, done in by literal fire rather than the figurative sort. Neal Cassidy (41), the real Dean Moriarty, was found in a coma beside some Mexican railroad. Joplin's (27) story is as old as time, while Kerouac (47) himself died of a hemorrhage caused by too much drink and, well...whatever else people choose to say a death is brought on by. Lonesome hearts and too many tears aren't figured into that equation, and neither are dark thoughts from outer space.

Gone-rogue galaxies without end.

Joan Baez (alive) was doing well in sunny Woodside, however, and that was enough to keep her going. Sometimes it's the exceptions that cause all the trouble, the outliers. False positives spoiling all the variables, creating hope where there should've been none. But hell, what did she know?

Sooner or later, we all end up in the ground.

"*Door's open!*"

Coda hesitated, and gave another few knocks at the door.

"*I said, come in!*"

"Hiya, Mr. Hal, can I open the door?"

Coda smiled to herself, wishing she had her broomstick to add another pair of knocks to the others.

"*Just go away!*" he called.

She barged in and found Mr. Hal staked out by his big bay window. The oxygen tank latched to his wheelchair glinted in the sun, gasp-gushing over the noise of the television in the center of the room. Coda glanced at the screen and saw some flat-looking show that had ended before she'd been born.

"Guess who's back?" she asked.

"It must be you."

"Ms. Wendicott says you could use a little assistance. Is that right, Mr. Hal? How are we feeling today?"

He stared back, studying her with an unknowable expression.

"Do you remember me, Mr. Hal? What's my name?"

"If you're here to work," he told her, "then work. If you're here to talk, then leave. Either way, I don't care."

"Okay, okay," she said. "Tell me what to do."

"I'm hungry, and I need meals. I can't do it myself anymore, and my nurse is woefully inept."

"Sure, I'll cook you anything you want. How about some grilled cheeses?"

"I need *instant* meals, yes? Something I can go right to the refrigerator and take out and eat. Right then! I need it to be easy. And then maybe I need some intermediate meals, something that might take a little longer. Two or three minutes. No longer than four, you understand? And some boiled eggs. My eggs are going bad and the stove makes me sweat. *Lots* of boiled eggs."

She would kill the old bastard before it was over. She knew it, right then.

"Okay, Mr. Hal. Sure thing. And how about that dirty laundry I smell, would you like me to do that, as well?"

He gazed out the window, the gasp of the oxygen tank marking the time.

"I'll never wear those clothes again," he told her. "I'll be dead by then."

"That's no way to talk, Mr. Hal. Let me wash them."

"Oh, you didn't know? I like the stench of my own dirty trousers. It's one of my favorite things."

"You should be locked in a freezer and froze to death," she muttered, and started away toward the bathroom, to the overflowing laundry basket outside the door.

"What's that?"

"*Nothing, Mr. Hal!*"

"I heard you, all right."

The hum of the motorized wheelchair filled the room, then the crunching of old Chinese take-out containers and diet soda cans as he plowed into the kitchen. Mr. Hal managed to pull a glass from the open dishwasher, and was struggling to fill it from the fridge's water dispenser when it fell shattering to the floor. He hit reverse, crunching over the shards of glass.

Coda watched him wheel into his bedroom, returning moments later with a checkbook. He scribbled out a check for two hundred dollars, handed it over.

"You can read, right?"

Coda took the check, staring at her name in Mr. Hal's terrible, nigh illegible handwriting. She leaned over, giving him a peck on the cheek.

"Believe it or not, I'll miss you when you're gone."

He looked at her, eyes scrutinizing the golden hoops in her nose, the flowering tattoo down the side of her face. The oxygen tank gasped, shuddering at the side of the wheelchair. Then he was gone, motoring back across the landfill of Styrofoam and Chinese take-out, into his room, slamming the door.

Later that afternoon, once she'd made his meals and boiled the damned eggs and cleaned his house, Coda left Mr. Hal in front of the big bay window where she'd found him. She'd managed to change his bedpan (without puking up her guts, no less), and even trimmed his hair and nails while he dozed.

He slept soundly in a morphine haze, and she patted his bald head before leaving. "Take it easy, old man," she said, and looked past him out the window, watching the street down below. She imagined what it would be like to watch this same street day after day, and decided it might not be half-bad with a bit of death-juice to pass the time. What is it they say? Youth is wasted on the young, and good morphine on the old.

She went downstairs to her apartment, and sitting at her laptop saw a message from Alex.

`<DROOGMANALEX: can you make it today?>`

<DROOGMANALEX: around 7pm?>

She checked the time on her phone: 5:17.

<CODA64: what happened to Friday?>

She stared at the screen, her anxiety ratcheting up as she waited for a response. Then it came:

<DROOGMANALEX: something came up. you want it or not?>

<CODA64: see you then :)>

Alex read the message, relief flooding his veins.

It had been hours, and he was beginning to think she'd flaked on him.

<DROOGMANALEX: perfect. don't be late>

No sooner had he typed the message than his mother walked into his room, going to his mirror to check the look of her evening gown, plushing her hair, dangling the splashes of gold from her ears.

"Remember, don't answer the door," she told him. "I've left a pan of meatloaf and some salad in the fridge, in case you get hungry. Okay, hun?"

"Sure thing, Mom."

She turned to him, walking over to see him playing *Duke*

Nukem on the laptop. She kissed the top of his head.

"No scary games," she told him. "They'll give you night-mares."

Alex groaned, switching away from Duke and pulling up *Chip's Challenge* instead. "Yes, Mom..."

"Your father and I will be home no later than nine. Call us on your dad's cell if you need anything."

"Please, Mom. Don't be a spaz. I'll be fine."

"Hey, watch your mouth, young man. Your mother is not a *spaz*, okay? She just loves you very, very much. Now come on down, we're about to leave. Come tell your father goodbye."

"I'll be down in a minute, Ma," he told her, maneuvering Chip around the board, though he'd played this level a hun-dred times and could probably beat it blindfolded. But it was either that or Purble Place, and he'd whipped up enough cakes in that game. Not bragging, but he was basically the Betty Crocker of Purble Place.

His mother ruffled his hair, returning down the hall.

"Two minutes, Alex. Come down and say goodbye."

When she was gone, Alex closed out of the game. Their dinner party had come up last minute, and he'd decided to-night was the night. A happy accident. He grabbed the two remaining vials of his Halloween stash from the back of the drawer, stuffing them in his pocket.

Then he went downstairs to see his parents off.

CHAPTER FIVE

Coda left just after six, cruising the forty miles to Arcadia with a sudden itch that refused to be scratched, some dreadful fire burning from within.

With Alex's impromptu message, her night had blossomed like a ghostly moonflower with secrets untold, and she could hardly wait to get it started. Her nerves ran hot, arms trembly as she'd steered the car past the usual fuck-a-loos outside Finnegan's and took the highway toward Korova. If the old crotch-sniffer with the curdled-milk breath was in attendance, she didn't notice.

She arrived just before dark, once again pulling around back. She stopped just shy of the grass, her Corolla edging on the crumbled pavement. The corrugated tin shed stood ominously in the gathering dusk, the orange light from within now vanished and only darkness lining the old shed's walls.

Someone banged on her window, making her jump.

She spun, peering through the glass to see the same fucking toddler-boy from last time, a hardened stare on his face. Not a smile like other children, and not a put-on. A cold granite stare that seemed out of place on the young boy's face.

She dropped her window a few inches, cutting down her radio.

"Hey, listen, I told Alex no babies this time. What the hell, kid. Go back inside, tell Alex to come out."

"Be cool," the boy said.

"Listen, dude, just go get Alex, okay?"

He held up the vial, the darkness inside gleaming red in the fading light.

"Want it or not?"

Coda stared at the vial, flashing in the dying sun. She released a breath, reaching one arm out the window, the boy pulling away at the last second.

"C'mon, kid, cut the shit."

"Be careful with this batch," he told her, slipping the vial into her palm. "It's not like the other one. Stronger."

"Says who? *Droogman Alex?*"

He looked at her, and something had changed in his face. Just like that, in the blink of an eye. He was speaking past her, into another place.

"*Says me, okay?*"

She looked into his eyes, lost in a fantasy. Before she drowned there, sinking irrevocably into the pools of his dark-ocean pupils, Coda tucked the vial between her legs, her foot letting off the brake. She reversed down the crumbled driveway, the boy following her out to the corner. Then she jammed the car into gear and sped off, the weight of the boy's eyes heavy at her back.

He watched her go, eyes following the Corolla as it vanished down the street beneath a cumbersome umbrella of smog. Night crept closer, the sun already setting in a pool of burnished brass through the trees. Alex watched the branches twitching in the breeze, and realized he was twitching right along with them. The flesh of his face was misshapen, a melted too-long-in-the-microwave grimace, fingers plucking a strange tune on the harp strings of his heart.

He'd dosed only minutes earlier and the drencrom moved in fast, grabbing him by the throat.

He rushed back inside and went straightaway to the kitchen, grabbing some ice out of the freezer. He collected the cubes into a bowl, grabbing a dish towel and a couple rubber bands from the junk drawer. Some masking tape, and—remembering Halloween night—a couple more dish towels for good measure. Last of all, he grabbed one of the throwaway plastic grocery bags his mother kept in the bottom cabinet before heading outside.

And to think it all started with an allergic reaction to peanut butter.

That had been a close call, his parents said.

Then they'd introduced him to an epinephrine pen, and all that had changed. Being no dummy, he'd done his own research and learned a thing or two himself. All that information floating around out there, all of it flashing like shooting stars across the web and leaving footprints in modems the world over.

The entire planet was shrinking faster than ever, and nobody seemed to notice.

But he'd run across more than the effective administration of epinephrine, or the untold dangers of peanut allergens. He'd tumbled down one rabbit hole after another, until he knew unequivocally he'd never hit bottom. Then one night he'd stumbled over something *new*, further down the annals of human evolution. A reinvention of wheels beneath the engine of his ever-unfurling mind. They say the vast universe is still expanding, creeping farther into the untouched reaches of not-yet-matter, and he'd hitched his wagon to that rolling tide.

And then he'd come back.

A frontier revenant.

Better, stronger, more than human.

Then a new question had emerged: *what next?*

So he'd decided to branch out, freeing minds one innocent lamb at a time. He was a Johnny Appleseed of sorts, planting his liberation of earthly fear and desire, breaking them from the temporal cages of their oh-so-mortal coils.

Coda64 would be the first.

He moved out to the corrugated tin shed, hitting the lights and shutting the door. His father had set up the place as a kind of work shed, his tools and other things scattered about. The only thing lacking was the smell of sweat and sawdust, because his father spent about as much time out here as Alex spent in Paraguay. The stereo worked just fine, however, and presently Alex turned the dial, ramping up the noise of the classical station. Mozart's Requiem in D minor was in full swing, and he turned it louder still before moving to his father's workbench.

He reached back, fishing the blade from where he'd hidden it in the boards. He'd been meaning to clean it up a little, but cleaning the blade was never foremost in his mind after nights like these, and he always forgot about it afterwards until coming back for more. He brought the cruddy blade into the light, placing it next to the canning jars he'd grabbed from his bookshelf.

He arranged the items along the workbench, the drencrom pushing strong, his vision blurring. He pulled off his shirt, tossing it to the ground. His skin shone eerie-golden against the shed's orangish haze, the light burning down on him in waves, and he steadied himself. If he wasn't careful, he'd slip right out of his body as surely as he'd slipped out of his shirt, straight through the roof, and the whole thing would be for naught.

But he held on, edging toward the center of the shed where he'd set up the chair on top of a quilt thrown down over the earthen floor.

He sat down and grabbed the cheap grocery bag, thin enough to see through, slipping it over his head.

Then the rubber bands, bunching them together.

A three-strand cord, he'd learned, is not easily broken—even in the throes of death. Once upon a time, getting those bands around the crown of his head had proved a challenging feat indeed. Nowadays he slipped them down in one graceful motion, the rubber bands clenching tight around his neck, tying off the bag.

His breaths had grown heavy, the blue grocery bag covering his face and the drencrom flooding his vision, making the world an ocean of waves. A riptide clawing at his eyes, turning dark at the edges as the music swelled and his hand reached out, snagging the blade from the workbench.

He'd begun to thrash, his small twelve-year-old body fighting hard for survival. He fumbled the jar, knocking it across the workbench, then grabbed hold and pulled it close before dragging the blade along the scarred flesh of his chest. Low, just beneath the ribs. The adrenal glands sat atop each of his kidneys, two taps from a life-giving fountain. He jabbed roughly, ripping a fresh wound. The warmth of the blood spilled down, wrapping him like a mitten, and he collected the sap of himself into the canning jar.

Then gasping, the blue wall closing in. Darkness ringing the edges of his consciousness like a tunnel straight to hell, a sunken abattoir of fear.

He slashed again, the rugged blade catching on the very pores of his skin. The blood burbled out of him like a stream, flowing deeply now, filling the jar. This first runoff was less potent, he knew.

He'd have to go deeper for the good stuff.

Alex reached out, arms juddering as he slid the jar roughly onto the workbench. He grabbed the second jar, the bag clinging tighter at his skull, wrapping him like a mummy, suffocating, and then everything opened up and the expanse of the universe filled him, sliding between his skin and that of the world. Then a massive creaking like the walls of an old house settling as something joggled loose and he rose through the ceiling, beyond the roof, higher into the clouds.

The town of Arcadia glistened down below, the homes and cars like fireflies across the night. He gasped in the wind, filling his lungs. His eyes focused past the clouds, and he saw the riders out there, like stallions of fire galloping across the night, and struggled to take hold of himself.

He pushed himself down, sinking, sinking, back down into his twelve-year-old self. His adrenaline was spiking, everything coming into focus. He remembered the knife in one hand, and the canning jar, and promptly ripped the blade in a sweeping arc across his flesh. A thick dark crude spilled out of him, brimming the jar.

The good stuff.

He'd managed to join this jar with the other on the workbench before tearing out of the bag, gasping, slippery ropes of slaver hanging from his chin. More blood slipped past his waist, dripping down and staining the quilt beneath the chair. He grabbed the first jar, topping it off from his wound and then taking a gulp, refilling it. He made a small noise under his breath, what he'd intended as a laugh but which came out instead like a last, desperate gasp for life.

The eternal music of Mozart roared like lions from the stereo, spinning the dross of a dying world to purest gold.

CHAPTER SIX

Coda rushed inside her apartment, slamming the door and locking it.

First things first, she went straight to the computer.

```
<CODA64: WTF i said no more KIDS>
```

```
<CODA64: ass>
```

Unbelievable.

But she didn't have time to think about that.

Later, maybe. Not now.

She quickly undressed, keeping an eye on her laptop. She abhorred the pageantry of going out in public, the cavorting and carousing. Worse than this, she hated it even more when she actually indulged herself and played it up a little, sticking it to the bitches (that part she loved). Overall, she found beauty boring. Boring and banal and totally played out.

Today, however, she'd indulged herself, getting all dolled up (a relative term—she didn't go to the nines for *any-fuck-ing-body, ever*) and now regretted it, dragging herself out of her stylish jeans and chains, the tall post-goth girl platform shoes, taking out the barrettes and letting down her hair.

She slipped into her pajamas, snatching the vial from where she'd left it beside her laptop. She checked the screen— no response from Alex—before moving into her darkened bedroom, standing before the mirror.

She sat on her bed and drank down the vial, gagging at that same acrid taste. This one was goopier than before, a dark coagulate that slipped thick as molasses down the back of her throat. She gagged, almost spitting up, and got hold of herself.

She stared at herself in the mirror, the room still dark.

She'd left her window open and a cool breeze brushed inside, rustling the curtains. Only the little nightlight near her bathroom glowed, seeding sparkles in the eyes of the girl in the mirror.

Then the *rush*.

It swept down her body, a warm tide of some unknown sensation filling her completely.

She shuddered, stroking absently at her breasts. The darkened room lit up, dazzling her senses as she dropped a hand, grinding at her clitoris, until then the feeling paused, pooling warmly at the center of her being.

Another cool breeze through the window, and riding on the wind she caught whiffs of the food trucks parked downtown, the earthy stench of the woods, the smell of scorched engine oil.

Her make-up that afternoon had been immaculate—her eyeliner a tad dramatic, but hey, nobody's perfect—and even now the remnants drew her stare, forming her face into a perfect skull of sadness. She dreamed back at herself in the mirror, the rush of a thousand rivers coursing through her veins. She'd never imagined a feeling like this, had no way of figuring it into words.

Another warm rush, flooding from her head all the way down, a reverse-sensation of bubbles rising to the surface. She gasped. Her nerves popped and fired, twisting her awkwardly atop the bed. Her hands clenched, quivering, bunching the sheets.

She shook, but not the way she thought, not the way it *felt*.

Not physically, but everything inside of her had turned to cotton.

Her innards fuzzy and vibrating, tendons and sinews caught in a sudden whirlwind spiraling desperately from a drain at the bottom of her soul. And that whirlwind was all right—just fine—but what's worse, the quick beneath her fingernails had turned to candle wax and was gumming up her breathing.

She gasped again, moving faster than she'd ever known possible, flashing through some rough approximation of light-speed and never inching from the mattress. There was a shape in the mirror, staring back at her, and now the lips of the girl in the mirror were moving and she heard a raspy voice that sounded like a siren flashing red across the night.

The girl reached forward, clawing out of the mirror. The

glass bending in a certain slant of light, and when she looked next the shadow-girl had stepped down into the room and was running out the door.

"*No, wait!*" Coda called, scrabbling after her.

She came into the front room, and saw her door standing open on the dimly lit hall. The stench of scorched engine oil was overwhelming, hovering in corkscrews above the mealy hallway carpeting. She moved in that direction, stopping outside Ms. Wendicott's door. She knocked twice, her hand passing through the door, never touching. So she knocked again but now the door was open and Ms. Wendicott stared at her over a steaming cup of Earl Grey.

"Come in for tea, dear?" she asked.

Coda nodded, or meant to nod, but instead felt herself flushed into the apartment, swimming in the plushy cushions of the couch.

"You look absolutely radiant," Ms. Wendicott was telling her, pushing her steel-trap walker in circles around the room. "Have you seen my glasses, dear? I can't see a thing without my eyes..."

Coda stared, watching her cruise endless circles around the den, the gutted tennis balls of her walker dragging lines across the carpet. But the faster she went, the more copies of herself she left behind, a thousand afterimages of a thousand neon Wendicotts tearing ass across the floor. There was a racetrack here, Coda realized, and the real Ms. Wendicott was winning, running laps around the competition.

Something glinted and Coda turned, staring past the nothingness of life until her eyes caught the shape of the girl, her shadowed form grinning obscenely in the gilded mirror across from the couch.

It was herself, of course.

She was staring at some scorched-engine-oil-version of herself and nothing more, except in the gilded-mirror reflection she'd crawled up into the ceiling and was dangling in some spindly unseen web. From Coda's position on the couch, the pair had locked stares and the girl hovered precariously, her mouth running a red siren and Coda stood suddenly, rushing to the window, gazing down into the wicked heart of the forest far below.

"Ms. Wendicott?" she asked. "Have you seen my shadow?"

She looked back and Ms. Wendicott had grown silent, huffing as she pushed the walker in faster and faster circles across the carpet, a thousand neon Wendicotts in hot pursuit. Coda hadn't realized it, but she'd taken a mint from the jar on the kitchenette table, and presently slipped it into her mouth; a cool mint rush swept down the runnels of her being, and with it she realized something else—namely, that she'd been wearing Ms. Wendicott's fancy cat-cye glasses around her neck this entire time.

She slipped them on, staring down into the forest.

The shadow-girl waited just below, her narrow reflection waving back from the darkened mouth of the trailhead. Coda raised an arm, veins cording tight as she reached down through the window, the grass tickling her fingers, the reflection performing a sudden insect crawl along the bristles of her arm, clattering up the bones of her fingers and then—

Coda spilled forward through the window, the two of them gathering into one along the tides of the wind. The horns of the universe were blowing all at once, and they were calling her name. She moved out over the tops of the trees, floating down among the streets of downtown and beyond. Through a flash of burning light, she peered through a glass darkly and saw Gaston Hughes behind the counter of his father's store. There was a figure in a mask, and shouting, and then sudden gunfire that crashed like lightning from the heavens. She watched Gaston, sprinting from behind the counter, and then a silver cord snapped and she stood at the window, looking down over the trees.

"Here you go, Ms. Wendicott," she said, pulling out of the cat-eye glasses.

She stared dazedly across the room, the sights and sounds rushing her all at once, clouding her mind and troubling her stomach. She hadn't noticed her cup of Earl Grey steaming on the little end table, the citrus fragrance of bergamot calling out to her, but the thought of drinking it made her nauseous.

"Oh, aren't you just a sweetheart?" Ms. Wendicott asked, strolling closer. She took the glasses and put them on, then returned to her seat, reaching for another warm sip of tea. "I believe I'd just about lose my head if it wasn't attached to my neck."

"You could never do a thing like that," Coda told her. "I know you better than that, I'm your daughter now."

Ms. Wendicott smiled. "Oh, I suppose we are a little bit like that, aren't we? You'd make any mother proud, dear. A smart, beautiful girl, the world would be a better place if there were more people like you, Coda."

Her reflection had returned to the mirror, but instead of the ceiling her shadow-self had taken up residence in the wall, hiding in an old Dutch painting of the countryside. She cried bashfully from within the stately frame, her dark tears streaming ink down the subdued yellows of harvest and completely ruining the Dutch handiwork.

"Oh, I didn't mean to upset you, dear," came Ms. Wendicott's voice. "Would you like more tea?"

Coda glanced down, lost in the empty cup in her hands.

She'd drank the Earl Grey in one gulp and never known she was doing it. Which would have been perfectly swell any other night of the year, but tonight she'd felt the shadow-girl crawling up her arm, and she'd lost and found herself in the Dutch countryside, and the rotgut tea had blossomed in her belly like the jagged fist of nightmares.

"No, Ms. Wendicott," she heard her calm response. "No, I'd better be getting back home. I'm not feeling so well."

Ms. Wendicott stood, shuffling over behind her walker. She reached out, wrapping both arms around her in a tender embrace.

Feeling quite frail all of a sudden, Coda returned the embrace, struggling to keep the worm of the shadow-thing from slipping out of her fingertips and scaling the old woman's legs, crawling inside.

She returned down the hall to her apartment, following the stench of scorched motor oil into the bathroom. She ran cold water in the shower, and was barely able to peel out of her clothes before stepping inside. The cool minty rush of the water beat down upon her and she retched awkwardly, the warmth of it slopping down her chest, chunking off her thighs. The minty smell soured, and when the second push rocketed from her throat, dousing the shower walls, some vitality went out of her and she sank to the floor, spiraling down the twisty hairball labyrinth of the drain.

CHAPTER SEVEN

Earlier that evening, his business having concluded in the shed, after he'd soothed himself with ice and calmed down enough to stand, Alex hobbled inside for a quick bath. After cleaning and bandaging his wounds, he'd went downstairs, swallowed some meatloaf, and whipped up an ice-cold pitcher of blueberry Kool-Aid.

Upon his parents' return, Alex had two special glasses waiting for them at the kitchen table. He'd added a little something extra to their glasses—not drencrom, they weren't ready for that, not yet—but something to make his night a little easier, uncluttering things.

Nights like these, he'd found it hard not to roam.

He climbed out of bed now, caught between the frailty of his vessel and the strength of the drencrom. The moon had grown purple through his window, neon shadows performing a sinister burlesque along the walls.

He moved down the hall, stopping outside his parents' room.

He peered inside, watching them sleep. He'd pumped them full of so much melatonin, they could sleep through a cataclysm. If the whole earth blew up tonight, they'd have to read about it in the papers tomorrow morning.

He stood for a long time inside their darkened room, considering them.

As parents, they were so-so. But then he was an only child, and Alex supposed he should cut them some slack. His father claimed he was conceived in space. Alex's mother, the story went, had been a stowaway on the shuttle—or, in other stories, old pops had spooged into a cup up there in orbit and the in vitro had been a success.

His father also told him his brain was off, because of the moon and all that space dust. From private conversations he'd overheard, his mother had doubled down on the subject. Oftentimes he'd looked without success into his father's closet, searching for his astronaut diaper. He knew all about the astronaut diapers. But he supposed his father had gotten rid of his, because it was nowhere to be found. Probably he'd stashed it away as a surprise sort of birthday gift when Alex was older, an heirloom. A very valuable astronaut diaper from outer space, lightly used.

He stepped closer in the darkness, peering at his father.

Why did you make my brain full of moondust?

Alex hovered quiet as a stone over the bed, watching his thoughts coalesce in a thunderstorm over their sleeping bodies. His father felt the rain down in his dreams, and when Alex tossed a thunderbolt down there, he heard his father's fearful dream-moans echoing up the chamber of his soul, and he laughed and laughed. Laughed until he no longer made sense, even to himself.

He'd never made much sense to himself.

Probably it was all that moondust his father had brought back in a cup, mixed with a mother who didn't just break the mold—she shattered it to a million-billion pieces. He supposed he was half-alien, and probably his own kids would be more spirit than flesh, floating on pixie wings with the new-fangled children of the future.

For a long time he stared at his parents beneath the covers, hanging on their furtive breaths. He wormed deeper into their thoughts as they dreamed, their sleeping eyes shut tight against the world.

Let me tell you a story.

This is the story of me and my parents, and what happened between us all those years ago. I haven't talked to them since, have never seen their faces beyond that night. Not one phone call, never a postcard.

I don't like to talk about it, so I'm only telling it once.

Cool?

For starters, let's just say it: I'm a bit of a handful.

I know it.

I'd really put them through the wringer for a couple years, and maybe I wasn't the model daughter they'd hoped for. They weren't pillars of morality themselves, don't get me wrong. Just, sometimes a parent might want their kid showing some ambition or making good choices, and that wasn't really my bag in those days. I'd dedicated myself to a whole different path, and maybe I was just being super patient with them until they caught on to that fact. I'm probably the single most patient person I've ever met, and undoubtedly the humblest.

Then one random weeknight I strolled up and found my father in his fancy rocking chair, smoking his stinky old cigar on the big front porch they'd built that summer. He stood when he saw me, walking to the front door.

"C'mon on in here, honey," he said, stepping inside. "Where have you been?"

I looked around, suspicious but half-amused. Like I'd been accused of sniffing undies. "Watching Joey for Mrs. Menders, Dad."

"Babysitting?"

I laughed. "Yes, Dad, babysitting. What's going on?"

"Come on in, sit down," he told me, and now I'd followed him up the porch steps and into the kitchen, the lights turned dark. I looked, and noticed my mother's shadow at the kitchen table.

"Why is it so dark?"

My mother switched on a light, and I saw her eyes were cold.

"Sit down, this instant."

"Coda, we've heard some disturbing news," my father told me. "Very disheartening, to say the least."

"What kind of news?" I asked. "Like, is somebody dead?"

The half-joke fell flat, only my parents' stern expressions glaring back across the kitchen table.

"Have a seat," my father said.

I pulled up a chair, feeling awkward sitting there at the table with no food between us, no three-course meal. We were what most would consider fairly upper class, and were rarely all three of us in the same room unless it was mealtime.

"What is it?" I asked, all gooey-eyed innocence.

"C'mon out, Miles."

Mr. Rutherford shuffled out from the hall, eyes on the floor, his hat in his hands. He walked over to the table, taking a seat beside my father.

And just like that, I knew the score.

The jig was up.

"Miles, would you tell Coda here exactly what you told us earlier?"

Mr. Rutherford glanced at me, his eyes looking sorry as hell.

"You approached me at the corner, where I was drinking," Mr. Rutherford told me. "Where I always drink. I'm a brown-bagger, I admit it. Not proud of it, but that's what I am. And you came over and said, well..."

He looked ashamed, staring at the table.

"Go on," my mother said.

"Well, you told me you'd...you'd pay me six hundred dollars to tie you up, right there in the alley. That you had the rope, and you'd pay me good money to tie you up and strangle you."

"Mom-Dad-that's-not-true! He's lying!"

I was lying.

He'd mixed up the language, but he had the gist of it.

"And then what happened?" my mother asked.

"When I said no," Mr. Motormouth went on, "you showed me the money, wagging it at my face. Begging me, for all the booze in the world. Told me how you wanted to die, and you'd do anything for it. That you wanted me to throttle you."

Damn, Mr. Rutherford had a swell memory for such a boozehound.

"Mom—Dad—I've never seen this man—"

"This is for your own good, Coda," my father said, cutting me off. "We take no joy in this. But you're eighteen now, and even though you've wrecked your car, we believe it's time you found out what it's like to be on your own. Your things have been packed."

"What? You're not serious?"

"You have one hour to gather any items we might've missed, and to make arrangements. We've thrown out your drugs, so don't bother looking for them. And don't phone the police. We can lie as good as you—much better, in fact."

"Guys, I'm scared. Stop this." I did my best at groveling, reaching at the ceiling like I'd gone suddenly blind. "I don't know what's happening."

"You have one hour," my mother repeated.

"Can I—may I go now?" Mr. Rutherford asked.

"Of course, Miles," my father said.

Now, I guess some kids might have hard feelings about that sort of thing—I mean, pretty extreme right? Tossing your kid out like that, for basically no reason at all. But I like to think they'd finally caught on, my parents. That I wouldn't have to waste any more time exhausting my patience, or casting my pearls before swine.

I'd won.

And the funny thing about all this?

The funny thing is, even after my dismissal, I was blocks away, walking the back alleys out of town, before letting myself smile. Freedom is hard to come by sometimes—the hardest—and I'd taken a lot of shots at it before. A part of me couldn't believe it. A part of me still can't.

What can I say?

What's meant to be will always find a way.

PART TWO

"Adrenochrome," he said. "You won't need much. Just a little tiny *taste*."

I got the bottle and dipped the head of a paper match into it.

"That's about right," he said. "That stuff makes pure mescaline seem like ginger beer. You'll go completely crazy if you take too much."

I licked the end of the match. "Where'd you get this?" I asked. "You can't buy it."

"Never mind," he said. "It's absolutely pure."

I shook my head sadly. "Jesus! What kind of monster client have you picked up this time? There's only one source for this stuff..."

He nodded.

"The adrenaline glands from a living human body," I said. "It's no good if you get it out of a corpse."

Hunter S. Thompson
Fear and Loathing in Las Vegas (1971)

CHAPTER EIGHT

When Cutty Suggs walked into the apartment, Trent was reclined on the couch, studying a vintage radio system service manual. The TV was on, the volume blaring some Sarah MacLachlan tune, and Cutty sat down, staring at the screen. There were animals in cages looking miserable, and he realized Trent was watching one of those slow-motion sepia-toned animal rescue shows.

"What's this?" he asked.

"What?

"Why do you watch this stuff? You like looking at these tortured dogs?"

"Oh, I'm not even watching that," he said from the couch, the yellowed service manual perched in his lap. "That's just white noise."

"Well, then why don't you *change the channel*? I don't

want to see that crap when I walk in here. I don't want to see a bunch of pit bulls with their fuckin' faces hanging off their face, buncha sad-sap monkeyshit. Turn it to Lifetime, Weather Channel, anything, dig?"

"Fine, fine, stop bitching."

He held up his hands. "I'm just saying, bro. Turn the channel if you're not watching it."

"Grapple Fest is coming on later. Wanna watch? Bucky's got a match."

"Bucky the Brawler?"

"Bucky the Brawler, sure enough."

"I used to love Bucky the Brawler. Who's he fighting?"

Trent yawned. "Nintendo Kid."

"Shit, I'm down. Wanna make some magic brownies?"

"Don't you have an appointment tonight? You know, that thing with Gaston? Like, committing felonies or whatever?"

He waved it away. "Aw, that's not for hours. Let's get dirty-dirty."

Trent flipped another page. "All right then, sure. Oven's over there."

So they baked some magic brownies, chomping down on the edibles as the announcer appeared at the center of the squared circle and bellowed his signature *Let's-get-ready-to-GRAPPLLLLLLLLLE!!!* and the crowd went apeshit.

It was a big night for pro wrestling, the biggest of the year. Grapple Fest was the crème de la crème of pay-per-views, and thanks to Trent's hacking prowess the month before, they were getting it for absolutely zilch dollars. This being the case, Cutty might have gotten a little heavy-handed with the special sauce and the brownies came out potent as a swift kick to the groin.

They chowed down as a pair of ladies took to the ring, slamming each other around like rag dolls. *Damn*, the boys kept repeating, punch after sloppy punch, slam after slam, *damn*, chomping away on the brownies as the ring turned red with blood. Grapple Fest wasn't like those other sissy wrasslin' shows, and more often than not things got nasty.

"Damn, that hurt."

"Damn, girl. Coochie-kick, watch out."

Pretty soon the ring looked like a slaughterhouse; the ref, caught in the thick of it all, began vomiting profusely all over the mat. Minutes later he counted the 1-2-3 and the match ended and the ladies hobbled backstage.

An hour later the stadium lights went dark and Bucky the Brawler was set to square off against The Nintendo Kid. The match was a nail-biter, involving ladders, ringside chairs, a judge's mallet, and an electric egg-beater. But when the Nintendo Kid performed his Up-Up-Down-Down-Left-Right-Left-Right-B-A finisher and Bucky was pinned for the first time in Grapple Fest history, the edibles kicked into high gear and the night took a turn for the worse. Cutty was in a dark place, snacking away at some nachos and cheese in an attempt to kill the high, when his phone buzzed and he saw it was 8:56.

"*Shit!*"

"I know, I cannot fucking *believe* it," Trent said. "Bucky should've took him out after he broke that Game Genie Death-lock."

But Cutty had gathered his things, grabbing his bag from the couch. His mask was inside, along with a burlap sack he'd brought along for the money.

"I'm late," he said, rushing for the door. "Gaston's gonna

flip!"

"*Don't get murdered!*" Trent called, but Cutty barely heard him.

He ran downstairs, hopping into his car and peeling out.

Minutes later he pulled into the convenience store parking lot, gasping for breath after all the close calls he'd imagined on the way over. The edibles were kicking his ass, and whenever he looked out the window there were ghost-faces peering in from the darkness. He'd almost struck a pedestrian jaywalking, banged over a pothole and knocked the alignment all to shit, and had not once but *twice* stopped at a green light.

He parked at the back of the lot, checking the time: 9:07.

He pulled up Gaston's message from minutes earlier: WTF ARE YOU??

He texted back: HERE

Cutty searched inside the store, spotting Gaston behind the counter. Chandra, the other attendant on duty, was next to him, the two of them laughing. They moved to look at the glazed donuts in the little display and Gaston fished one out, splitting it with her. Cutty checked his phone.

Nothing.

Before their donut was finished, an elderly lumberjack-type moved into line and Gaston went to take care of him. Three scratch-offs and a six-pack later, the lumberjack was moving out the doors and Chandra had vanished into the back.

His phone buzzed, a message from Trent: UM DID YOU FORGET YOUR WATER PISTOL??

Cutty cursed, shaking behind the wheel. He'd spent a lot of time painting that water pistol, then greasing it up to shine just right. Now what would he do? There was no time to go back—

Another message, this one from Gaston: NOWWW

Cutty grabbed his ski mask from the bag, slipping it over his head.

He grabbed the burlap sack.

Then, searching the darkness of the car, the edibles grabbed a nerve in his brain and he sprang forward, grabbing his old paintball gun from the backseat. He kicked open the door and hurried across the pavement.

Make it believable, that's what Gaston had told him.

He burst through the doors, brandishing the paintball gun in front of him. "*Give me the money, pantywaist!*" he shouted. "*Give me the money now or I'll execute every motherfucking last one of you!*"

He aimed the gun at Gaston behind the register, who looked as if a seagull had dropped a full load down his mouth. His friend stared back intently, whispering under his breath: "*SHUT THE FUCK UP. THE CAMERAS CAN'T HEAR YOU, DUMMY.*"

"*Oh, shit,*" Cutty whispered back. "*Sorry.*"

Gaston pretended at trembling, opening the register and filling the sack Cutty passed to him over the counter. He said, "Is that a paintball gun?"

Cutty shrugged.

"Please, please—just don't shoot, mister," Gaston recited, stuffing the money into the sack. "*You imbecile, a paintball gun...?*"

"*Yo, can I get some Doritos?*" Cutty whispered.

Gaston shook his head, the anger burning in his eyes.

He kept stuffing, stuffing.

"Every last dollar, you unwashed butthole," Cutty said.

Gaston held back a smile, filling the last of the bag and handing it over.

But Cutty was getting into it now, brandishing the paint-ball gun around the store. He snatched the bag and said, "Don't make me pump this store full of lead, dig?! Don't make me—"

He stopped.

He'd turned slightly, facing the beer cooler in the back. Except there was something very wrong happening in the beer cooler, because that girl Coda-something was standing back there inside one of the glass doors, her reflection wavering, eyes locked on his in a laser-beam stare.

But not only that—she appeared to be...*was she...*

Floating?

Suddenly the front door shattered, crashing to the floor.

There had been a noise, some explosion from the side of the store, and a second explosion thundered loudly as he turned and saw Chandra standing outside the stockroom, a pistol—a real fucking *gun*—clenched in one hand.

The plate glass window at his back shattered, and Cutty jumped, the paintball gun going off and spraying a ball of ne-on-purple on the far wall.

Cutty hauled ass.

He leapt forward, plunging through the remaining slivers of glass in the door, an icicle shard catching him over the eyes and drawing a line of blood down his ski-mask.

"*I'm gonna kill him!*" Chandra roared, sprinting toward the shattered plate-glass window. Gaston cut her off, holding her back and telling her to stay down, get away from the windows.

"*Not again, not on my watch!*" she shouted, and blasted another shot through the shattered window. Hearing the shot from outside, Cutty—who by now had hopped inside his car and was peeling out of the lot—promptly lost his bladder, groaning as he jumped the curb and sped into the night.

"*No-no, stay calm!*" Gaston told her, pulling the gun away from the window. "*Stay calm, I'm calling the cops! It's okay, stay calm!*"

"I'm calm," Chandra said, lowering the pistol. "I'm calm, I'm totally fucking cool, okay? I'm good."

"You good?"

Chandra looked wired, but closed her eyes, breathing in and out.

"I'm *good*."

Gaston released his own heavy breath, looking around the store.

What a mess, he thought.

He glanced once back toward the beer cooler, where he thought Cutty had seen something—something that stopped the words cold in his throat.

But there was nothing there.

Moving slowly, Gaston Hughes walked behind the counter. He spent a few minutes feigning a search for his phone and then, pulling it from his pocket, reluctantly dialed up his father.

CHAPTER NINE

When she woke that next morning, the water had washed everything clean and Coda felt like a million bucks twice over. The shower was still running, a low pressure, cold-as-ever drizzle. She stood, shivering, and rubbed on some soap and rinsed and then stepped from the shower, and already she'd noticed daylight creeping in through the windows.

Early morning, she thought.

Minutes later she'd made some wheat toast with Vegemite and settled at her laptop, memories of the night playing in her head. She logged on and got to work.

```
<CODA64: I need more>
```

She waited, remembering the flight she'd taken out of Ms.

Wendicott's window, the sprawling lights of downtown, the weeping girl inside the painting. She couldn't get it out of her head. After half an hour, she decided what she really needed was to cleanse her mind as she'd cleansed her body.

She'd read once that being near open water significantly improved a person's peace of mind, increased their relaxation. That sense of awe, she supposed, just from being around those crashing waves: the sounds, the smells, the rush of cool breeze sweeping in from the sea. She didn't feel much like going down to the pier, however, and the downtown fountain had quit-out last fall.

She considered this, staring at the screen, waiting for a response.

Well, shit.

Finally she got up and ran some lukewarm water inside her tub and added some Morton salt. When it was finished she stood staring at the water, waiting for all that peace to come floating down like butterflies. When that didn't happen, Coda decided maybe she'd need to up the ante here. A bit of wildlife would work wonders, she thought, and considered a visit to the disco couple down the hall. If they had a couple spare goldfish, she wouldn't mind dropping some inside, watching them splash around while she got all peaceful.

But she felt like visiting the disco couple even less than driving down to the pier, and so Coda settled for what she had and flushed the toilet for aural stimulation and pulled up a chair.

For a long time she sat staring at the water, trying to relax. Imagining the seagulls in her mind. But standing water in a tub didn't seem the same as a real ocean, not at all. The peeling wallpaper kept drawing her attention, the cruddy tiles glistening with grime. The gloopy, calcified remains of her vomit spotting up the wall. She hated it, all of it. She felt anxious, like she wanted to grab the tub and rip it from the floor.

Then the chime of a notification from her laptop, and she leapt out of the chair. She ran back to her living room, sighing heavily at the sight of Alex's response. She sat down, and began to type.

<DROOGMANALEX: When?>

<CODA64: now, tmw, idc>

<CODA64: now>

<DROOGMANALEX: hmmm>

<CODA64: what?>

<DROOGMANALEX: just thinking>

<CODA64: I'll pay double>

<DROOGMANALEX: Friday then>

<CODA64: what time?>

<DROOGMANALEX: I'll let you know>

CHAPTER TEN

But he hadn't let her know.

Two whole days had passed, and still no word.

Hours earlier, she'd sent him another message:

```
<CODA64: hey we still on for today??>

<CODA64: send out the kid if you want idc
lol>
```

Now here she sat on the cusp of another shitty weekend in Hagerstown, waiting for a message she felt might never come.

The sun sank lower, drawing the shades on the sky. She'd visited with Mr. Hal in 4-C the previous evening, and Ms. Wendicott for a few hours that morning. Now she had three hundred bucks in her back pocket and a long Friday night ahead. As it stood, if things got much worse, she'd probably end up walking down to One-Eyed Jacks for a game of pool, or Tramell's for some backroom poker action, though she'd never cared much for Tramell's.

She'd lit some incense, grabbing her Morton salt and drawing some lukewarm water into the bath, when her laptop chimed. She ran over and read the message twice, staring at the words. Something shifting down inside of her.

```
<DROOGMANALEX: come now or forever hold
your peace>
```

She was on the road in less than two minutes, speeding along to Arcadia.

When she arrived, pulling around back, the same kid came out to greet her. Moving slower this time, with a slight stagger to his step.

"Heya kid, you okay?"

He held out his hand, reaching inside the open window and dropping the vials into her lap. "Two-for-one sale," he said.

She looked at them. "This the good shit?"

"Same as last time, sure."

"How much?"

He leaned closer, a different sort of fire in his stare.

"Alex says it's on the house."

She didn't like the sound of that. Nothing's free in this world—and of those things that *seem* to be free, black-market drugs are nowhere on the list.

"What's the catch?"

"No catch," he said, staring past her to the corrugated tin

shed. "Alex says he's getting out of the business. Consider it a parting gift."

"But...what if I want more?"

The boy shrugged. "Go ask Alex."

Coda went to open her door and the kid grabbed hold, gently shutting her in. He peered at her, a distant look in his eyes.

"Not here," he said. "Later, online."

She looked at him, that same funny feeling coming over her again.

"Tell him I said thank you," she said. "For the freebies, I mean. Take care of yourself, kid."

She reversed out of the driveway, backing into the street. When she looked next, the boy stood in the last of the day's light. Staring. He lifted a hand to wave but she turned away, keeping her eyes on the road ahead.

The road goes on forever.

Then one night you wake in a hospital, broken on the wheel of too-fast living, but don't bother sticking around. You raise all kinds of hell, ripping the lines from your veins and storming out into a fresh North Dakota blizzard. You push through the whipping wind and snow, finding an alley and letting yourself down, shivering against the breeze.

And right then, with Big Dean and Lady Zelda over your shoulder—and that old guard of tramps out on parade, bugling a perpetual chorus of CARPE DIEM—you finally make peace with Emily Dickinson.

The Myth of Amherst, she who rarely left home and secluded herself from rabblerousing society, from the road and all its curbside vanity fairs. She who shut herself off from the long arm of the general populace, and yet from her private chambers produced those golden seeds that fed the world.

It was not a life you'd ever hoped for, an anathema to all you'd held dear.

But sometimes the road takes uncertain detours.

Unlikely destinations unknown even to ourselves.

The mad ones, the burning ones, who never said a commonplace thing—they're fun for a while. Just like, don't live too long, or one day you'll wake up dead or—perhaps—uncommon in a very different, not-so-fabulous sort of way.

Some things are worse than death.

CHAPTER ELEVEN

"So I talked to your bestest-buddy Cutty today."

Gaston bit back his anger, his hand gripping tighter at the phone. There were a handful of people he absolutely, positively did *not* want Cutty Suggs talking to right now, and his brother Knox ranked near the top.

"Oh yeah?" he asked, playing it cool.

"Yeah, I'd been looking for him a couple days now," Knox told him. "Ever since I heard Daddy's store had been robbed with...what was it? A *paintball gun?* Hell, I understand the sonofabitch even got off a shot or two. Big ball of neon-purple paint, right there up over the beer cooler."

"Knox, what the hell are you talking about?"

"Cut the crap, Gaston. Me and Cutty used to ping squirrels with those things back when you were still in diapers. Should've known I'd find him down at the old railroad, same old Cutty. Living it up in that beat-up old Chevy. Fucking four-door motel on wheels."

"It wasn't Cutty," he said, trying to sound sure of himself.

"Oh yeah?" Knox said, and he was giggling now. "That's not what Cutty said. Matter fact, he told me all about how the whole thing went down—what was it he said? Oh, that's right. That it was *your* idea. Even better, that you got half of the take. Now how about that? Sure would break old Dad's heart to hear a thing like that, his own son setting him up and all."

He let out a breath. "C'mon, Knox. Be serious."

"Oh, I'm being serious. So unless you want me to clue Dad in on a couple things, I'm gonna need to feel the love myself."

Gaston groaned. *Fuck-fuckity-fuck.*

"How much?"

"Half of what you got."

Now the groaning had turned to laughter. "Get the fuck outta here, half. I'll cop you a hundred, but that's it."

"Half, or I'm telling Dad."

"Good, then you'd better tell Dad you tried to skim half a score you didn't have nothing to do with."

"All right, if you say so."

"Fuck off, Knox."

The line went dead.

Gaston lowered the phone, thinking. He turned, his eyes falling on Trent sprawled across the couch.

"I won't say I told you so," Trent yawned, watching the Weather Channel and flipping through another dusty Sherwood manual.

Gaston grunted, gathering his keys and walking out the door.

The old Tangiers railroad ran just through the woods out

back of their apartment, so close he normally walked out a couple times a day to check on Cutty. But right now, after that phone call, what he needed was some time alone. He peeled out onto the highway, blaring the radio as he cruised out toward Cullen, picking up some greasy drive-thru before turning back. He took the old logging road down to where Cutty had set up camp.

"Here, got you some burgers," he said.

"Thanks."

"How's the shoulder?"

Believe it or not, Chandra Sykes—the girl with the gun—hadn't been such a bad shot after all. The bullet had only skimmed him, little more than a flesh wound, but that didn't mean it didn't sting like a bastard. It had bled all week, and now Cutty was wondering if that wasn't the reason for his dizziness, his lack of appetite.

"Hurts like hell, if I'm being honest," he said. "Not exactly a six hundred dollar wound...but no take-backs, I guess."

Gaston strolled over, leaning against the old Chevy.

"Heard Knox dropped by."

Cutty looked away. "Yeah, I guess so."

"And so what? You *told* him? What the fuck, Cutty?"

"Ahh, he already knew. I swear it, Gaston, he knew the score as soon as he saw me laid up back here, with all this blood everywhere."

"Well, now he's threatening to tell my dad."

Cutty looked alarmed. "You think he'd really do that?"

"No, not really," Gaston told him. "Just lay low out here a couple more days. I'll keep a watch out, but nobody knows nothing."

"Except Knox."

"Except Knox, yeah." Gaston tossed over the bag of burgers, his eyes sweeping the dark swaths of blood stained along the Chevy's seats. He shook his head. "Had to bring that paintball gun, didn't you?"

They looked at each other, starting to grin.

Cutty massaged the wound in his shoulder, pretending he was a soldier just back from war. "Magic brownies, man," he said. "Fucking magic brownies." Gaston had started away when he called to him: "Hey, there wasn't anybody else in the store that night was there? I mean, besides Chandra?"

"Nope, just us," Gaston told him. "Why?"

Cutty stared out into space, considering.

"No reason."

CHAPTER TWELVE

The incense had been burning since she left and now the smell of patchouli was almost cloying as she settled on her bed. Coda held the vials in one hand, clenching them warmly to her chest. She'd sipped gingerly from one as she walked through the door, and presently the first rush of drencrom took hold, turning her fetal on the mattress.

Her legs quivered, juggling the laughter from her throat, and when the quivers had faded she sat up, drinking down the rest of the vial.

When she looked next, a bounding wind had spilled inside the window, spinning the last smolders of the incense across the room. She watched it, feeling another sort of wind spinning inside of her, some crucial element from within spiraling in all directions at once.

She slipped out of her body, floating higher toward the ceiling.

Gazing down, Coda observed her body relaxed supinely on the bed, eyes glassed over in some peaceful, cascading reverie. Her attention shifted to the weathered gray bureau against the wall, and she noticed her reflection-self leaning expectantly forward beyond the surface of the mirror, watching her ascent with dark, storm-cloud eyes.

Then the mirror-girl turned, staring toward the window.

She beckoned her down, her red-siren mouth flashing in the darkness. Hands flailing, gesturing to the open window, the slanted beams of moonlight mixing with the breeze and rushing steadily inside. Following her gaze, Coda observed the spectral figure of a young boy swept in with the wind.

The kid, she realized.

She pulled herself lower, hovering next to the illusory form—a form, she thought, not much different from her own. She lingered next to him, feeling faint in the darkness.

"*Now you know what I am*," the boy-form told her, his voice cobbled by the wind. "*And now you know what you'll become.*"

She hesitated, her vision blackening at the edges.

"*Alex?*"

His bushy head tipped imperceptibly, a play of shadows and light.

And she understood. She'd known it that afternoon, without knowing how or why. She couldn't understand, and understood perfectly.

He stepped closer, his naked body shimmering, wavering like a TV station too far to be picked up. She noticed the ragged scars low under his chest, just beneath the ribs. They'd healed and been ripped, again and again, the scar tissue bunched in fleshy ropes across his skin.

"*You said you wanted more,*" he told her. "*But you have everything you need. Everything, in here,*" he said, touching a small hand to the freshest of the scars.

"*How...?*"

He roamed closer, the hand moving from his wound and reaching out to her own flickering form. He touched her then, and she *understood*. She understood what she had to do, how the answer had been within herself all along. She just didn't know it. Didn't know how to reach down and collect it, how to make a harvest of herself.

"*Do you see?*"

She nodded, gasping for breath. Stumbling from his touch, wavering in the cool breeze through the open window. Behind her, the reflection-girl moved furtively inside the mirror, inspecting the borders as if for a weak spot in the glass. Some channel, some hidden beam of light to ride out into the world.

"*You won't see me again,*" he said.

"*Where are you going?*"

He glanced out the window, across the darkened heavens. In the distance, the fiery riders waited on the wings of the wind. There were so many of them, scattered like a ghoulish banner along the horizon.

"*Remember what I've shown you,*" he said, and when she looked next he'd been carried outside the window, swept away like fog over the waters of a swampy bog. She floated closer, the skeins of a silver cord trailing her approach, unspooled from the vessel of herself atop the mattress.

She gazed across the night, watching the boy-form swim skyward, saturating the cusp of the heavens, her own reflection crawling out of the mirror at her back and slipping quietly out of the room. The ghoulish banner of riders had shifted, stretching toward some indeterminate point in the darkness of space. The stars glistening, lighting their way.

Then only darkness, and the clattering of bells from outside her room. Small silver bells, clashing and clanging as she funneled surreptitiously toward the mattress, slipping inside of herself. She sat up, her head feeling woozy, but not so bad as to stop her from jumping out of bed, rushing to the window.

The usual stains of Hagerstown smog lay across the night, obscuring the stars. If there had ever been a highway into the heavens, then it had surely collapsed. The sounding of bells caught her attention from below, and she noticed her shadow-self down at the edge of the forest. The yawning mouth of the trailhead was too far to be seen from her window, but she watched the girl moving in that direction, her dark smile mixing with the shadows of the trees.

Coda turned, grabbing the last of the vials from the dresser.

She tipped it back, the warm syrup of the Alex-child's blood draining down her throat. She gagged, held it back, and when the vial was empty she bolted from the room, following the stench of scorched engine oil down the stairs and out into the night.

CHAPTER THIRTEEN

Across town at the Hughes residence, a phone rang.

Martin Hughes moved into the den, lifting the receiver of the old cord phone hung on the wall. It was the only cord phone in a sixteen-mile radius, probably one of the few remaining cord phones in the country.

Martin Hughes was more than proud of the fact.

"Hello?"

He paused with the receiver pressed against his ear, listening.

He grunted. "And who am I speaking with?"

There was an audible click over the line.

He glanced at the receiver, and hung up.

Cutty Suggs, he thought. That's who had knocked over the store and, if he wanted, he could call and report his ass right now. According to the voice on the phone—a woman, he thought, but couldn't be sure—he'd been bopping around town spending cash like it was going out of style. Which was rather unusual for someone living out of their car.

He went to the kitchen table, having a seat. Thinking things over.

He could phone the cops, of course. Turn him in.

But then...

But then, dammit, what about Gaston? His own son setting up the robbery—and for what? For some fast cash? Maybe. Although Gaston did have the occasional bleeding heart, and more than likely Cutty Suggs had duped him into it with some sad-sack story. Probably said he wanted to get better, go to rehab. Stop slumming down by the damned railroad tracks.

Martin Hughes groaned.

He could see how this one would go from a mile away. Cutty wouldn't be arrested five minutes before he snitched on Gaston. Then what? Then he'd spend even more money he didn't have getting his son out of jail, lawyer's fees, court costs. Hell, it'd be cheaper to sit on it.

He harrumphed, dragging a weary hand down his face.

His own son, he thought.

Better to handle this in-house, if only for his wife's sake.

Of course, he could always take matters into his own hands. Mayhap pay Cutty Suggs a visit in his one-room Chevy...

CHAPTER FOURTEEN

Coda entered the woods, sprinting faster as the drencrom dropped heavy as a cannonball down into her gut and her vision blurred with a thousand unknown colors, the gradient hues of the night coming alive.

Without realizing it, she'd begun to shiver, which seemed strange with the sweat burning in her eyes and her hair soaked down her back. Her legs quivered and shook, sending her stumbling along the path.

She had to stop.

Coda paused in the darkness, gathering her breath.

Snapping branches, just ahead.

Farther along the trail, she spotted the shadow-girl in a stray beam of moonlight. Staring silently back at her now, her dark eyes curious.

Coda slipped from beneath the tree, edging out onto the path. Her shadow-self mirrored her approach, the two of them drawing nearer each other as the moon shifted behind a cloud and the world of the forest went dark.

When it happened, something else shifted and went dark inside of Coda, a sudden cramp dropping her to her knees. She moaned, a double-edged sword of pleasure and pain, ecstasy and agony, meticulously rending the secret parts of her soul. Her mouth opened, jawing madly at the sky, until suddenly something ruptured from within and she slipped past her teeth, rising higher above the trees. She glanced out, watching the city spin in a myriad of cogs and levers, cars and traffic lights, laughter and tears. At the edge of the blue-black horizon, a swarm of riders fled across the desert of the sky.

She swooped lower, dropping swiftly, back down through the trees and the ragged edges of her teeth and settling again within the house of her flesh.

She was vibrating again, juddering against the earth and straw, something else building deep inside. The moon crystalized, drawing fractals of ice down her vision and now the pain was worse, exploding from within. A starburst of energy spinning razorblades in her gut.

The cloud shifted again, shedding light along the path.

She looked down and her stomach had bulged, a morbid paunch that throbbed and squirmed. She moaned deliriously, her sensations amplified like a bullhorn to her nerves. She stood from her knees, staggering along the path.

"*Please, please...*" she spoke to the darkness.

Her belly trembled, the pain burning like fire.

She unbuttoned her pants and in a glimpse of moonlight saw her stomach swollen beyond all recognition. She hefted it in her arms, struggling as she carried the ponderous weight farther down the path until the pain wriggled deeper, moving around to her ass.

She wobbled unsurely, waiting, waiting.

She'd barely been able to get her pants down, her lacy panties dropped to her knees, when she doubled-over. Something ballooned in her ass, the burden of the weight doing a sudden about-face and exploding out of her. She felt some intense pressure relieved, surging from her in a sudden, riotous rush of burning diarrhea across the forest floor.

"*Ughhaaaaaaaa*," she groaned, and the night stood silent around her.

A warming puddle of excrement caked around her, and looking down she noticed the bulging mound of her stomach had retreated, funneling within and then wrestling out of her and into the world. Something solid—and *sharp*—suddenly dropped out of her, splashing into the shit at her feet, and she turned, glimpsing movement in the moonlight.

A shadow of something fled quickly, scurrying across the ground and into the trees.

Coda sensed the last of her troubles slipping out of her, splish-splashing to the ground—and with it the last of her pain. The ecstasy had returned, sweeping down her legs, wrapping her in stars. She stumbled, her knees weak, then quickly recovered and snatched up her pants.

She rushed ahead, following the unholy stench and then catching sight of its source through the trees, the thing that had crawled out of her. Small, low to the ground. Slick eyes glistening in the moonlight.

It saw her, and for a long moment everything was frozen.

She stared, the night growing still around them. Gazing

closer through the darkness, Coda shook with terror, so scared her feet trembled and fingers twitched and jittered, playing some invisible piano on the wind.

PART THREE

"We were sitting in the Korova Milkbar making up our rassoodocks what to do with the evening, a flip dark chill winter bastard though dry. All round were chellovecks well away on milk plus vellocet and synthemesc and drencrom and other veshches which take you far far far away from this wicked and real world into the land to viddy Bog And All His Angels And Saints in your left sabog with lights bursting and spurting all over your mozg."

Anthony Burgess, *A Clockwork Orange* (1962)

CHAPTER FIFTEEN

"Hey-hey, wake up in there."

Cutty felt a hand shaking his shoulder, and flinched back in pain.

"*Owwww*," he groaned, peering up at the shadow standing over him. It was Gaston's father, Mr. Hughes, and he had a funny look on his face.

"Mr. Hughes?"

"Sit up, Cutty. C'mon, sit your ass up."

Cutty lay stretched out in the front seat, a thin blanket draped across his legs. Mr. Hughes had come up and opened the door, and now Cutty did his best to pull himself up. He stared out, the form of Gaston's father leering back at him.

"What's going on, Mr. Hughes?"

"Well, that's what I was hoping you could tell me, Cutty. From what I understand, you and my son pulled a fast one and

I got my windows shot all to shit. But I'm not here about the windows. I'm here about the money you boys stole from me, and because if I don't get it back, there's gonna be hell to pay."

Cutty shifted in his seat, biting back the pain from his shoulder. "Mr. Hughes, I don't know what you're talking about, sir. To tell you the truth, I've been a little under the weather lately—"

"Save it, Cutty. I know all about it. Don't play me for a fool, I know all about the set-up, the split, everything. Don't make a jerk out of me, okay?"

Cutty stared at him, still shifting in the seat.

"Have-have you—talked to Gaston?"

"I'll deal with Gaston," he said. "Right now, I'm dealing with *you*. I know the haul was twelve hundred. I also know you got half of that. What's really tickling my ass, though, is how much have you spent?"

"Not much," Cutty said, not so sure of himself. "Not really. I've, well—I guess—"

"Wait a minute, I take it back. I don't give a damn what you've spent, couldn't care in the slightest. What I *do* care about is getting back what's mine." He stepped closer, glaring. "Cutty, this is the part where you rummage around in that little shitcan-on-wheels, ferret out my money, and—"

"I'm not kidding here, sir," Cutty moaned. "I'm bleeding, real bad-off. Seriously, I need a hospital. I'm in a world of hurt here, dig?"

Hughes laughed. "A world of *hurt?* Son, if you don't hand over my damn money, I'll show you a world of—"

Something leapt through the darkness, attaching itself to Hughes's face.

It happened so fast, Cutty barely had time to register what occurred; from where he sat, it looked as if a wet-slimed shadow had zipped out of the brush, obscuring the old man's face like a bad-weather cloud.

Except it wasn't a cloud, and by the rising scream from Mr. Hughes's throat, it wasn't a shadow either.

Hughes hit the ground, wrestling with the thing and rolling in the dirt, screaming, beating at it with his hands. Then a squishing sound, like a boot lowered on a toad, and the screaming went quiet. The hands fell away.

Something caught Cutty's eye, a glimmer of light along the ground, and he noticed a thick, rolling river of blood flowing down the hill toward his car.

"*Oh-shit, oh-shit, oh-shit,*" he repeated, and slammed the door.

He peered through the window.

Mr. Hughes jostled limply, the animal tugging at the meat of his turkey-gobbler neck. It was a small-bodied something, like an armadillo soaked in sewage from hell. The skin was slicked down, either matted fur or scaly crocodile flesh—but black as pitch whatever it was, and filthy besides. He could smell it even from inside the car, and when it reared back and Cutty noticed the odd length of the neck, the ears spread like the wings of a bat against the moon, he shrank back against the passenger door.

He sank lower in the seat, too afraid to shut his eyes.

Even more afraid to keep them open.

The glass of the driver door shattered.

The creature sprang forward, arms thrashing.

But Cutty had crawled out the other side, slipping from

the open door and taking off through the trees. He'd entered the forest when a cold sensation touched like a ghost on his neck, and then—moments later—the ghost became real. The fingers were cold and slimy, the long nails wrapping snugly around his neck.

He screamed, plowing wildly through the trees.

"*Help meeeeeeeee*," he squealed, and then the fingers loosened around his neck and something sank down the back of his pants. He felt it deeper, closer, crawling inside of himself, expanding. Something very painful was happening inside of him, and when he looked down his stomach had plumped, like a bloated beach ball with rats inside. He felt loathsome, his shrieks fading as the blood came pooling at the back of his throat, shutting off his voice.

His shirt split, and now threads of blood drew a painful map along the stretched-tight flesh of his gut. He stopped among the trees, he could go no farther. The pain was too much to move, the torture dropping him to his knees.

"*Damn*," he said.

A hollow rush bellowed through the darkness, the shit-gremlin appearing from the cavern that had been emptied in Cutty Suggs's stomach. A grisly stew of blood and innards met the earth with a splash, running hot between his legs, then touching warmly on his face as he tumbled forward onto the ground.

The shit-gremlin screeched wildly, slurping the blood like an unholy gruel. He was a messy eater, and void of decorum.

He did not finish his meal, instead following the whims of his appetite farther among the trees.

CHAPTER SIXTEEN

No matter how she tried shaking it, the image of those slicked-over eyes glinting in the moonlight wouldn't leave her mind. She feared no amount of lukewarm bathwater—with or without goldfish—would ever cleanse her of that shape among the brush, its prickly skin like a rugged skink and the sinister insinuation of razored teeth in its underdeveloped jaw.

Coda had seen enough.

She struggled along the path, retracing her steps back toward the apartment. The temperatures had crept into the nineties, transfiguring the woods into a sweltering jungle of shadows and fear. The drencrom had taken her completely, slipping her along the ground, her vision blurred, her movements performed from the deepest, darkest depths of the ocean.

She sensed herself floating, seeping out of herself and skyward to the stars. Gazing down among the trees, she watched her Coda-self sprinting furiously down the trail, a miniature doll on a string. Silver flashed in the moonlight and she returned, funneling down, the enduring taste of the wind overwhelming that other, more acrid taste at the back of her throat.

Remember what I've shown you, the Alex-child had told her.

She approached the edge of the forest, the trail opening suddenly and spewing her out. She paused just outside the trees, the moon vibrating in beautiful fans along the earth, crashing down in a collapsible tide at her feet. And something else. Her shadow, dancing to some unheard subterranean rhythm along the grass before her. Farther along, the apartment building rose in a perfect tombstone of shadow, blotting out the night.

Coda's eyes moved higher, pausing at the sight of Ms. Wendicott at her window, staring down in a baleful sort of way that stopped Coda cold in her tracks.

She stared at the old woman in the window, the desperate, gobsmacked glare behind those cat's-eye glasses. Her hunched, classic-Ms.-Wendicott silhouette outlined in a darkness deeper than death.

Coda raised her hand, performing an impartial wave at the edge of the forest.

But Ms. Wendicott only squinted harder, her face pressing obscenely against the window. Her glasses buckled, tumbling from her face.

"*Ms. Wendicott...*"

Her face crushed harder against the glass, the first telltale cracks splintering down the panes of the window. Coda stepped closer, her vision focusing on the bulging blue veins down Ms. Wendicott's face, her pallid features turned soft as putty as they pressed harder still at the glass and—

The window shattered, dumping the old lady outside into the night and sending her plummeting below. It happened in the blink of an eye: the sudden, awful shattering of glass, and—just like that—the heavy crunching of flesh and bones pounding at a solid, unforgiving earth.

Coda's shadow turned, leaping away into the trees.

She ran to Ms. Wendicott, bending low to shake her, turn her over—

She stopped.

The bones had crumpled in her face, smashed together in an unnatural shape. Everything was flat, angular. Her skin had cracked, shattered like a teacup. Blood ran from the fissures in a dark and heavy tide, washing down into the grass. Coda held the woman in her arms, shivering like a fugitive riding the rails as the clouds made an endless mask of faces over their heads, morphing scowls of comedy and drama and everything in between.

"*You should have kept all those things to yourself, Ms. Wendicott,*" she whispered to the woman's bludgeoned head. "*Some things you have to keep to yourself, you can't say everything out loud.*"

Her shattered cat's-eye glasses hung from the strap around her neck, swinging across her matronly bosom as Coda turned her to the moon. Her nose had splintered in a sloppy sideways-nub smashed inside her face, and presently Coda stared at the hollow, struggling against a free-fall down inside Ms. Wendicott's empty head. She'd been running her entire life, but she'd never expected to end things here, sheltering herself from the world inside an old woman's cracked-to-hell head. Coda soberly decided she'd make the best of things inside Ms. Wendicott, doodling cave drawings along the contours of her dead-lady thoughts, waiting until the skull could be properly excavated and her rantings deciphered beneath a restorative brush.

She reached out, slipping the glasses from the mushy slope of Ms. Wendicott's neck. She put them on, doing her best to perch the cracked frames across her face. Staring through their shattered lenses, she noticed something that hadn't been there before. Some kind of leakage; a dark river unspooling from beneath the old woman's Sunday-best dress, stretching heavenward in a dark, insubstantial beanstalk to the stars.

She breathed deep, the stench of scorched engine oil heavy in the air.

Coda stared higher, following the smoky tendril that didn't quite touch the stars, but instead performed a sudden corkscrew inside the broken window of Ms. Wendicott's room, coiling inside the building and—

Two coarse-haired ears, thin as bat's wings, appeared from inside the window. They moved slowly, inching closer into the night air, the moonlight drawing a map of veins along their tender flesh. Then the knobbed-over skull, the shit-grem-lin with his tiny slack-jawed mouth, tongue lashing the blood smeared across his craggy lips. The slicked-over eyes peered down at her, glistening, their gazes kissing briefly along the tenebrous stalk—

—and then he vanished, returning inside the room.

Sonofabitch.

Coda stood shakily, tossing the glasses to the ground.

She moved around the building, entering from the door around back. Memories of the Alex-child flashed in her mind, the mottled ropes of his scars pulsing in the moonlight. She staggered up the stairs, struggling to tamp down her emotions, to somehow calm the torrent raging deep within. Ms. Wendicott had been good to her, that much she knew. She'd cared enough to welcome her inside, to talk with her and—more importantly—to *listen*. She'd made damn fine Earl Grey tea.

She deserved so much better than this.

Coda pushed inside her apartment, heading straight for the large misericorde blade on her bookshelf. In medieval times, she'd learned, stiletto blades like this were used to deliver mercy blows to mortally wounded knights. It was thin enough to slip through the armor, and she considered it would damn sure be long and thin enough to drive a fatal blow straight through a shit-gremlin, no questions asked.

The drencrom flared as she took the misericorde into her hands, the narrow blade glowing masterfully. She'd had her own ideas for the weapon, though even now couldn't be sure what form they might take. Evisceration is a strong word, but it had always come easiest. Now, seeing the blade burning in a violet haze within her hands, she knew that would have to wait.

She marched out, and was moving along the corridor towards Ms. Wendicott's door when she heard a sudden crash from the other end of the hall. She turned, and saw Trent collapsing into the wall outside his apartment. He scrambled back, struggling to his feet and falling again, his voice rising in an unintelligible murmur, a screech, a moan.

"Trent!"

He turned, saw her standing there in the darkened hall.

He staggered closer, finally gaining his feet and closing the distance between them.

"Trent, what the fuck?"

"*Gaston—*" he choked. "*He's—dead. I found him on the couch…and some in the kitchen. And…oh fuck, I think that was him hanging from the ceiling fan.*"

"Are you sure it was him?"

He raised one trembling hand, peeling back his fingers to reveal a severed ear, the bearded skin of a face flapping off the end. Gaston's sparkling faux-diamond piercing glimmered like a dusky jewel from the lobe.

"Damn," Coda said. "You should call the cops, probably."

He looked down, noticing the stiletto blade.

"Where are you going with that?"

"To kill a shit-gremlin. Wanna come?"

"What about—what about Gaston?"

Coda shrugged. "If it's any consolation, I'm pretty sure the shit-gremlin murdered Gaston. I mean, before he went to Ms. Wendicott's."

He looked at her. "Ms. Wendicott? She's…gone?"

"Do what you want," she told him, continuing down the corridor.

"Wait! Just two seconds, don't move," he said, and sprinted away, returning down the hall to his apartment. As she waited, a soothing warmth swept down her legs, buckling her knees. She quivered, shakily grasping the wall to steady herself. Opening her eyes moments later, Trent had reappeared down the hall, swinging a pair of nunchucks.

He sprinted back over, giving her a serious look.

"Okay," he said. "Let's do this."

"Such gallant pageantry," Coda told him, rolling her eyes. "P.s., aren't those illegal?"

He shrugged. "Only in California."

Then, on second thought: "Hey, Coda? Um...what's a shit-gremlin?"

But she'd already turned, walking away, the misericorde still burning bright and melding with her hand. Like a talisman, but more dangerous. Her mouth had become one with the blade, and from this same blade she sought the rending of goblin flesh and drinking of goblin blood.

They approached Ms. Wendicott's door, finding it open on the hall.

Not such a surprise, and neither was the skein of smoky tendrils from inside, trailing out of the room and farther down the hall. And though he couldn't see it, Trent caught the stench and breathed deep, the smell of scorched engine oil making him dizzy.

"C'mon," Coda said, pushing down the hall.

She followed the trail, watching as it dipped inside several other rooms, the doors pushed open. Glancing inside 3-F, the meaty remains of the disco couple had been stacked like cast-off lumber beneath the aquarium, a fleshy cairn that to Coda's eyes burned bright like a pile of red-hot coals. Overhead, their massive mirrorball flashed ominously, beaming terror-visions into her head.

"Coda," Trent said, tugging her arm. "Let's go..."

Moments later they'd reached the end of the hall, the last door before the corridor widened onto the stairwell. Like the others, the door was open but this time there was shuffling from inside, pots and pans. Coda glanced at Trent, and Trent made a face, anxious. He raised the nunchucks, swinging them over one shoulder into the classic starting position. Ready to pounce. Coda poised the misericorde, ready to glut herself on pure unadulterated goblin suffering.

She stepped inside the apartment and promptly noticed a thin man in overalls, dead on the floor. His throat had been gashed, ripped open, the raw crude of his blood burbling down his chest. Stepping in beside her, Trent saw it and gasped, and the ripped-neck man's better half exploded from the kitchen.

The nightgown she wore had been badly torn, and as she fled across the apartment, sinking into the shadows of an open door, Coda noticed the widening stain of blood around her ass. Her stomach had pulped out, writhing morbidly beneath the lacy gown.

"It's okay!" Trent called. "Ma'am, we're here to help!"

Trent moved closer to the darkened room, relaxing his posture.

"We need to get everybody out," he told her. "There's something very wrong here..."

"Trent..."

He patted his hand, hushing Coda quiet.

Now he was at the threshold, peering into the darkness.

"Ma'am, it's okay to come out—"

Trent's head exploded.

A blast of gunfire had come from inside the room—and now a second followed, ripping the long blond hair out of Trent's head, tearing the scalp from his skull. He watched, stupefied, as the blood poured out of him, shocked by the urgent rush of it from his flesh. As if his body had been but a temporary hindrance to this raging deluge of red tides, loosed now from his body by a moon so much stranger than our own, so much more powerful.

Trent turned, his eyes meeting Coda's across the room.

In that moment, Coda thought, he looked like a lost little boy, a toddler who'd wandered away from his mother and realized it too late. He stumbled on his feet, and when a third shot flashed from inside, Coda sprinted forward. She grabbed Trent, who slumped dead in her arms. She pushed back into the darkness, using his body as a shield until a fourth shot boomed, the muzzle flash lighting up the room, and Coda took her chance.

She plunged forward in the neon darkness, an afterimage of the flare lighting her way as she raised the misericorde and then swiftly brought it down. The blade landed a solid blow— where, she had no idea. But it was soft, and it moved, flinching away from the strike, and when she stabbed again, the touch of warm blood drew flowers on her face.

The gun flared once more, the blast booming in her ears.

But the shot was wide and the tide had turned, and she kept the blade in steady motion, like a lumberjack cutting down the biggest, ugliest oak in the bunch.

The victim of these blows had slumped over, collapsing beneath her.

She straddled the shape, burying the blade deeper into the neck—and that's when she heard another sort of boom.

Something exploded out of the woman.

It exited beneath Coda, the woman's chest heaving like all the air had been let out. There was a low suckling sound, then a terrible slurping as something dragged across the floor at her back. Coda spun, turning in time to see the staggering silhouette of the shit-gremlin, his tiny form lumbering awkwardly in the open door. By the dim light from the kitchen she noticed the scruff of a small beard stubbled on his chin, his scaly flesh rippled with warts.

He turned, sensing her stare.

Coda tumbled from the body, her hand touching on the floor—and the pistol in the dead woman's hand.

His eyes glimmered in the soft light, his malformed mouth splitting in the mockery of a smile. Between his legs, the probing nub of a peek-a-boo phallus dipped and swayed.

Coda gripped the gun in the darkness.

Moving slowly, very slowly.

She spun, aiming the gun, a sudden blast lighting up the room and—

He was gone.

She bolted to her feet, running out the door. Stumbling over Trent's nunchucks, she tumbled clumsily forward and then picked herself up to see the goblin's diminutive shadow fleeing into the hall, the noise of his tiny talons clacking up the stairs.

She lunged after him, the pistol clutched tight in one hand. She was halfway up the stairwell before realizing she'd left behind the misericorde, an image of Trent's head blossoming in blood replaying in her thoughts. The rush of the drencrom was losing its vigor, the world becoming too real around her.

The smoky tendrils had faded, growing dim.

Faintly, she noticed the last of them moving onto the fourth floor.

She exited the stairs, moving quietly down the darkened

hall. Another flare of drencrom and now the tendrils became clearer, coiling farther down the hall and into an apartment, the door canted open.

A rectangle of golden light shone from within, coloring the darkness.

She stopped outside the room.

Apartment 4-C.

She stared at the gun in her hand, though it was nothing like the misericorde blade. There were no spectral lights here—only the black tumor of death, gathered in a cloud around the weapon.

She stepped inside, noticing Mr. Hal's wheelchair across the room.

The wheelchair was empty, abandoned by the bay window. The oxygen tank gasping ominously in the stillness. Once more the floor had been covered in refuse, garbage, empty food containers. All of her hard work quickly undone.

Then another sound.

She heard *chewing*.

Someone snacking in the kitchen, just around the corner.

She crept forward, peering around the side.

Mr. Hal stood at the oven, his eyes dazed. He stared vacuously into space, naked except for the funny diaper he wore to keep himself contained. The diaper was drenched in blood, sopping down his legs, and he was busy cramming boiled eggs into his mouth, one after another. Crumbled egg tumbled down his chin, bouncing off the hairy bloat of his chest.

Not the normal kind of bloat.

The kind that squirmed and sweat, and burbled deep like the bowels of hell.

"Mr. Hal?"

He stopped chewing.

His eyes shifted, stopping on her.

"Remember me?"

Mr. Hal opened his mouth, the half-chewed eggs slopping down his neck. A terrible screech ripped out of his throat, and he broke into a run. Not at Coda, but toward the big bay window across the room. He sprang forward, leaping wildly onto the sill, crashing into the window; the glass shattered, swept away into the cool night air.

Coda raised the gun, her hand trembling.

Their eyes met, and Mr. Hal opened his mouth, lips peeling back in the grim mockery of a smile. Then, even worse, the guttural call:

Screeeeeeeeeeeeeeee—

Coda pulled the trigger.

CHAPTER SEVENTEEN

Click-click.

No bullets.

Click.

Not even one fucking bullet.

The gun was empty and Coda stood motionless as the grimace slipped from Mr. Hal's face, the ghoulish screech fading to a whisper. The sweaty bloat of his chest shifted, dropping down into a paunch in his gut, then shifted once more, crunching and grinding into his back. Something wriggling from inside. A shivering, sweat-sheened hump that rose like a knot from his flesh.

His arms thrashed, shattering the rest of the bay window.

A cool breeze swept in from the night, washing the greasy stench of the downtown food trucks over to her in the kitchen. The food trucks, and something else. High metallic, with a tinge of shit.

Mr. Hal's diaper.

She dropped the gun, staring at the heaving, breathless form of her neighbor perched on the ledge. His eyes glimmered darkly in the moonlight, like ripples off a pond, drawing her to himself.

Coda fought back, struggling against the invisible strands between them.

She had made this thing, and now it deigned to unmake her.

An image of Ms. Wendicott surfaced in her mind, the taste of her mints, the warm smell of her honeyed Earl Grey tea. Coda snapped back, funneling as if from a great distance into herself, and the bond was broken.

Mr. Hal tipped forward, plunging out the window.

"No, Mr. Hal!"

But rushing to the window, she saw he hadn't plummeted like Ms. Wendicott. Instead, she watched his shadow floating away on the wings of the wind, his diapered, bulbous form moving effortlessly across the night sky. Coda stared through the broken panes of the big bay window, the last of the coiling tendrils mixing with the smog until one was unidentifiable from the other. For an endless moment, Mr. Hal soared among the clouds, his silhouette shrinking away against the shivery glow of the moon.

Then he was gone, vanished into the night.

CHAPTER EIGHTEEN

Coda woke on Huxley Beach, tucked away beneath the pier that, for the past few weeks, she'd called home. Seagulls swooped overhead, chittering away beneath the burning sun. Things weren't as bad out here as people thought, and moving from downtown had been the best decision of her life.

Not that she'd had much of a choice.

Not after they'd condemned the building, after all the crime-busters swept in and the place got cordoned off like Chernobyl. Nobody could say for sure what happened, besides an obvious bloodbath. A tragedy, with no clear culprits and just as many suspects. Especially since she'd high-tailed it out of there, had left Mr. Hal's and gotten herself dolled-up in the nearest gas station restroom and spent the rest of that night sticking it to the bitches at Tramell's.

Nobody knew what happened, and she wasn't speaking up.

She reached over, the noise of the ocean and the gulls swelling around her as she rummaged inside her bag, grabbing the two-liter of rainwater and washing out her mouth. Her throat tasted of hangover—not vomit, but very stale. Drencrom, she'd found, had a different sort of hangover than other highs. Once she'd gone astral sailing, surfing among the stars, and the next morning could barely stand or even walk straight.

She'd replaced the two-liter when a sudden wind rushed beneath the pier, stopping a newspaper on her blackened foot. In the fading daylight, she could make out the headline: SEARCH CONTINUES FOR MISSING CHILD.

She leaned forward, ignoring the flare of pain from everywhere at once, snatching the newspaper before it could be carried off with the breeze.

ARCADIA—Last month, Melinda Burgess and her husband, former astronaut Gordon Burgess, experienced every parent's worst fear when their twelve-year-old son, Alex, went missing without a trace. At present, little can be known, and law enforcement authorities are asking—

Before she could finish, another cool breeze rushed along, lifting the paper from her hands and whisking it away. She wasn't much for running these days, or even walking, and so instead she rummaged once more and took another sip from a different sort of bottle, gagging at the acrid taste.

She'd taken a second swig when Coda slipped out of herself and went coasting along the rays of the setting sun, surfing the broadheads of daylight on her way to dusk. She was seeking something out here, and came swooping low over the downtown bars, sleazing among the crowd. She sifted them thoroughly, rolling their thoughts like marbles in the palm of her mind. The smell of scorched engine oil had proven evasive, teasing her, always at the tips of her fingers, the blackened edges of her vision.

But she was determined.

She snapped back into her vessel, gasping for breath.

There were two men standing over her, gaping like the dunderheads at Finnegan's or One-Eyed Jacks. Their clothes were ragged and muddy, buttons missing from the one fella's flannel shirt. If not homeless, Coda figured, then trending right along in that direction.

No-Buttons raised a finger, pointing to the blood pooling out of her, a place just beneath her ribs. They couldn't see the ropey scar tissue, painful with every breath. Neither did they notice the pair of toes that had been severed from her left foot, or the deeper incisions beneath her breasts.

"You've hurt yourself, gal," he told her, and then the old fool actually grinned, his buddy joining in. "You'd better plug that up, y'hear?"

She studied them, their vacant stares growing dim at the arrival of dusk. The blood puddled beneath her, stretching across the sand to their worn-out soles, and now the grins faded from their faces. They stepped back, whispering. More than anything, they seemed terrified at the sight of her.

She wondered how much more terrified they might be should she reach out, burying the misericorde into their guts.

Just below the ribs, say.

She wondered what a thing like that might taste like.

She wondered how much deeper she could go.

What can I say?

Nobody gets it figured the first time, that's why life is so long.

That's why mistakes happen, and regret is the best recipe for perfection.

And sometimes, even wrong turns can take you back home.

Looking down most nights, swimming among the stars and those fiery riders standing sentinel across the heavens, I've witnessed a people done in by the consumerism of a frivolous life. Easily earned and easily spent, with no refunds. No returns of investment. The cankerworms had spawned, gestating in their own unique ideas of success, and now the metamorphosis was complete. They've kinged themselves, knitting fresh caps as the queens of empire and commerce— power brokers, the oil of the gears of the world. The ghastly, unkempt machinations of eight billion souls under heaven. Minus one, Ms. Gladys Wendicott. Minus two more, a disco couple neatly stacked in hellish kindling, ripe for the fire. Minus nameless others, for a grand total of eight fucking billion moths to the flame. Eight billion clandestine mortals with an itch to scratch, now rubbed raw on the underbelly of desire.

In another few billion years our sun will burn out, expanding and collapsing and casting a frozen earth to go it alone in deep space. And where would that leave them? All those beautiful, tragicomic souls, flittering like fireflies in the gloom of coming winter, serene and eternal, a dream from which humankind can never wake.

Will it ever make sense?

I'm not so sure.

Sometimes making sense of it all is a sure-fire path to insanity.

But that's why I keep pressing on, keep playing the odds.

Somewhere out there, something lives that needs to be put to death.

That night in the woods, I gave birth to a thing that can never have a name. Something feral, that haunts and roams, and takes the people we love. Sometimes it wears their faces. Sometimes, I think if I can only seize it with my own two hands, it'll never be free to hurt anyone ever again.

Meantime, what can I say?

What's meant to be will always find a way.

AFTERWORD

When I first set out to write *Drencrom*, my only goal was to create the clearest, most concise story possible, void of all murkiness and totally without guile. A real crowd-pleaser. The kind of tale that spurs a modicum of water-cooler talk, enough to down a couple paper cups or perhaps a proper decaf.

Okay, not so much.

I was, however, fresh off the heels of another manuscript, with enough left in the tank for one more detour. The themes of duality and Lynchian symbolism related to that previous book carried over into this one, but coming out of novel country and into the novella badlands, I decided to take the brakes off. Have some burnout, freewheeling fun, without preamble or apology. I've written another afterword to that other book (it's called *Boomerang*, a sort of woodsy, psychological horror novel that hopefully makes its way into readers' hands sometime within the next ten years), and while I won't recycle that afterword here, there is one point that bears repeating.

As with all of my longer works, *Drencrom* is the amalgamation of several influences and inspirations, many origin points that spread a map in my mind. For *Drencrom*, like *Boomerang*, the most prominent of those included filmmaker David Lynch. While *Boomerang* focused more heavily on his seminal TV series *Twin Peaks* (and for inquiring minds, see Episode 29 re: scorched engine oil), *Drencrom* took another page from his playbook—namely, leaning generously into the notion that a work should speak for itself, no matter how strange or daunting. Lynch has been notoriously evasive concerning the interpretation of his films, and I thought it would be interesting to indulge a more nuanced, intuitive approach to storytelling. The clues and symbols are all there for in-depth consideration (should that be your fancy—paradoxically, I believe these stories should be readily enjoyed as surface-level entertainment), though the uncovering and deciphering of them should be trusted to each individual reader, as we all bring our own rich storehouse of ideas, memories, and dreams to the thought-worlds we create and consume.

With that being said, I hope you've found something worthy here of carrying back home. If not, then I suggest grabbing some Morton salt and filling the tub, putting on some calming music ("Ride of the Valkyries" or Beethoven's Ninth, perhaps), and enjoying some boiled eggs by the water.

Hamelin Bird
April 2023

ACKNOWLEDGEMENTS

Many thanks to all the friends, fellow freaks, readers, and reviewers who continue to support my work, especially those who have been there from the beginning. Likewise, much appreciation to the horror community at large, my IG family, and all of those future readers who give my stories a chance.

I'd like to specifically shine a spotlight on author A.A. Medina, a true creative who served as cover artist and overall designer for this book, as well as *Wayward Suns*, the mass-market paperback edition of *Double Vision*, and my story *Hideaway*. His artwork is unparalleled, and his patience everlasting.

If you aren't yet familiar with his work, go and check out Fabled Beast Design.

Furthermore, I'd like to thank the many other fellow authors who have shown their support, and taken the time to offer advice, guidance, and friendship.

ABOUT THE AUTHOR

Hamelin Bird is the author of *Double Vision*, which *Publishers Weekly* called a "creepy nightmarish debut," *Wayward Suns*, and the stories *Woolie* and *Hideaway*. He lives and works in North Carolina.

www.hamelinbird.com

ALSO BY HAMELIN BIRD

WAYWARD SUNS

"Bird's prose sets the bar high for his contemporaries in this slice-of-life tale marbled with self-destruction and ambiguous hellfire magic. Smart, deep, and honest. Highly recommended."

—CHAD LUTZKE, author of *Slow Burn on Riverside* and *Of Foster Homes and Flies*

The year is 1987. Before the end of the Cold War, before O.J. and the L.A. riots and the World Wide Web. Hair is big, excess is in, and Weston Mercer is slowly losing his mind.

Then he meets a stranger who reveals things, dark things. Things Wes wishes he never would have heard. In the shadow of these darker truths, nothing can ever be the same...

Love. Addiction. Music. Death. Sex. Obsession. Madness.

ISBN: 978-1735489162

ALSO BY HAMELIN BIRD

DOUBLE VISION

"Bird's creepy, nightmarish debut...keeps readers off-balance as he builds toward a satisfying conclusion. Fans of thrillers with a supernatural tinge will be pleased."
—*Publishers Weekly*

For fans of Stephen King, Ronald Malfi, and Lawrence Block, Hamelin Bird delivers a compelling meditation on addiction and fatherhood.

Former detective Michael Lunsmann is about to lose everything. Still in love with his ex-wife, estranged from his teenage son, and now fresh off the wagon once again, rock bottom has never felt closer. But things are about to get worse. Following another Father's Day disaster with his son, Lunsmann wakes from a drinking binge with a bullet in his arm and no earthly idea how it got there. That same night, four teens go missing at the hands of an elusive madman.

Drawn into the investigation, Lunsmann launches an effort to catch the killer. But to repair the damage to his family, he'll have to confront his own demons. When the most unlikely detective becomes the only man to crack the case, dark and sinister forces will stop at nothing to prevent the truth from surfacing.

ISBN: 978-1735489155

ALSO BY HAMELIN BIRD

WOOLIE

A SHORT STORY

"I hit the gas and took the turns, thinking about where would be a nice place to stab somebody if I really had to, someplace that would hurt like gangbusters but that wouldn't kill. Only I'd never learned that far in school, where to stab somebody I mean, and figured just so I avoided the neck and didn't go too hard things would be all right."

THE KIDS AREN'T ALRIGHT...

A starry night glistening across the water. A weekend opening in a spread of angel's wings, calling the feral hearts to dance. The cold touch of beer brings the night alive, and everything goes black.

Follow our humble narrator on a reckless journey of teenage bacchanalia, decadence, and dope, from the banks of the bluffs to the place where blood is spilled, where the nights turn homeward to madness and death is always near. In the end, it's just another weekend on the edge.

Life in the fast lane. Dance on fire. Don't lose your head.

"A few weeks earlier we'd drank too much Crown and sat up all night with a couple friends, talking about all the plans we'd made in the past three months to kill ourselves. She'd planned on doing it with a pair of lethal T-cuts to her wrists, while I'd planned on driving down to the bluffs and blowing my head in with a shotty filched from my girlfriend's dad. Only then on the Big Day I'd heard "Tonight, Tonight" by The Smashing Pumpkins on the radio and got so excited about doing myself in that I got happy and backed out. So had Crystal, but I think her decision had something to do with getting her period."

AVAILABLE NOW ON KINDLE UNLIMITED

ALSO BY HAMELIN BIRD

HIDEAWAY

A SHORT STORY

In the tradition of *The Twilight Zone* and Thomas Ligotti, Hamelin Bird delivers a surreal tale of one man's perilous descent into madness—and, just maybe, his own place in a fractured world.

Meet John Eberhart, age twenty-nine.

Occupation: assistant to the vice-president, ad agency, Miro-caw County, Missouri.

His workday starts like any other—a splash of coffee, fol-lowed by early morning gridlock and smog and honking horns. But this morning, John Eberhart has taken an unex-pected detour. When he spots the Hideaway motel at the side of the road, he stops for the night.

But the Hideaway is a lot older than he could ever know, and the town in which it exists is not printed on any maps...

AVAILABLE NOW ON KINDLE UNLIMITED